Praise for
Mossbelly MacFearsome and the
Dwarves of Doom:

'Fast-paced action, zany characters, oodles of humour
and a touch of *Discworld* in an energetic fantasy debut'
THE BOOKSELLER

'Rollicking rambunctious plot and
realistic characters'
IRISH TIMES

'Fast-paced, smart, and very, very amusing'
SAM GAYTON

'Featuring memorable characters, a fast-paced
storyline and witty narrative, this book
is hard to put down'
NORTHERN YA LITFEST

MOSSBELLY MACFEARSOME

AND THE GOBLIN ARMY

ALEX GARDINER

ANDERSEN PRESS

First published in 2019 by
Andersen Press Limited
20 Vauxhall Bridge Road
London SW1V 2SA
www.andersenpress.co.uk

2 4 6 8 10 9 7 5 3 1

British Library Cataloguing in Publication Data available.

ISBN 978 1 78344 904 0

Printed and bound in Great Britain by Clays Ltd,
Elcograf S.p.A.

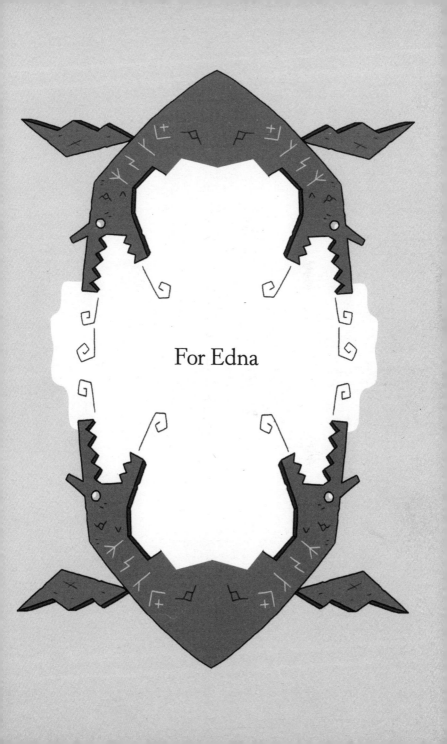

For Edna

Prologue

'Still no word from our tracker, Bloodbone Knottenbelt?' Queen Gwri looked at the High Judge.

'Nothing, your Majesty,' said High Judge Turbid Syllabub. 'Bloodbone is always reliable, one of our best. But there has been no word from him for several days. And we have read reports in one of those human paper-tablets of shrieking and strange blue lights emanating from his last-known area.'

The Queen glanced seriously at the other dwarf in the room, before addressing the High Judge again. 'And you think this means that the Goblin Chief has returned to Yester Castle to open the portal?'

The High Judge nodded gravely. 'Since the goblin Redcap was accidentally released from his incarceration by the human children, Roger and Maddie, the trackers searching the lands far and wide have found no trace of him – until Bloodbone's last message.'

Queen Gwri lifted the small piece of paper from the table in front of her. She held it close to her eyes. 'I cannot make out this writing; it is blurred from wetness. You are certain that it says, "I have found him"?'

'Yes,' said the High Judge.

Gwri nodded, then turned to the third dwarf. 'You know what this means?'

'I do.' Captain Mossbelly MacFearsome's face was grim. 'Our wedding ceremony is delayed – again.'

'More to the point, the portal!' snapped the Queen. 'Everything indicates that Redcap has returned to the area of Yester Castle. And the blue light could mean that the dodecahedron is already in place! If this is so, the portal will open at midnight on All Hallows' Eve and the accursed goblins will invade Earth, once more!'

Moss pulled his shoulders back and slapped his chest. 'I shall now go to do the impossible, in the shortest possible time.' He turned to leave.

'Wait,' said Queen Gwri, following after Moss on her backward-facing feet. She placed a hand on his arm. 'Take the children and the Witchwatcher with you. They must be involved in this for their part in the goblin's release, but inform them of the danger, the terrible risk. Protect them.' The Queen raised her other hand and gently touched Moss's beard. Her face was grim. 'The portal – it cannot be opened.

Not again! You understand the consequences should this happen?'

'I do,' said Moss, looking into the dark eyes in front of him. 'Death and destruction would follow.'

'Or worse,' said Queen Gwri, 'much worse. Now go, with all haste. Stop the portal from opening. Destroy it.' She broke eye contact with Moss and looked down at the floor. 'And in case something goes amiss, I'll be ready to recall the army from the north. The polar dragons could not have chosen a worse time to go on a rampage.'

Moss bowed. 'I shall not fail. Farewell.' He turned on his heel and walked out of the Queen's chamber. The door clicked shut behind him.

There was silence for a few moments.

'Ahem,' said High Judge Syllabub. 'May I leave as well, your Majesty? Only thing is . . . you're standing on my cloak.'

The Queen did not answer. She stared at the closed door, and spoke quietly to herself. 'I fear that it is already too late . . . much too late.'

CHAPTER
One

Miss Runacres was talking, but Roger was only half listening. He was lost in thought, miles away. His lack of attention had nothing to do with his teacher; he liked Miss Runacres and enjoyed her lessons. Roger was thinking back to when he and his friends had saved the world from the evil dwarf Leatherhead Barnstorm and his deadly gorefiends. It had been a great adventure – but terrifying at the time.

It was now the end of October, and he had last seen his friends during the summer holidays, when he had started his training as a Warlockwatcher at Auchterbolton Castle. Not that he had done much training or acquired any knowledge of even the simplest spells; he had spent most of his time playing games with Lady Goodroom's legally-adopted ward, Maddie. Lady Goodroom had been too busy looking after her husband who was recovering from his gunshot wound. And Wullie, now working full time for Lady Goodroom, had been busy overseeing the builders working on the wrecked library.

But now Roger was about to see all of them again. He glanced at his watch; in slightly over two hours Wullie was coming to pick him up at the school gates and take him to Auchterbolton Castle for Halloween. His backpack, with a change of clothes and Halloween costume, was hanging beside his anorak in the cloakroom. He was very excited and finding it difficult to concentrate on his lessons.

Roger rubbed his forehead – he felt a slight irritation – and began thinking about the one who had launched him into his great adventure after their accidental meeting: Captain Mossbelly MacFearsome, the grumpiest, most troublesome, aggravating . . . strongest, bravest, *maddest* dwarf he had ever met. A dwarf with the ability to turn pebbles into gold and words into nonsense, the one who had named Roger as 'Destroyer', a name he was secretly quite proud of.

Roger gradually became aware that there was silence in the classroom. Miss Runacres had stopped talking. He blinked his eyes and looked round. To his utter astonishment he found that he was standing up. The teacher and the entire classroom were staring at him.

'Roger?' Miss Runacres smiled, and then waited expectantly.

'I need to go – *now!*' Roger heard himself speaking, but had no idea why he'd said the words.

'Fine, Roger,' said Miss Runacres, slowly nodding her head. 'But you know that you don't need to stand up, just raise your hand when you need to go.'

'I *don't* need to go,' said Roger, feeling very bewildered. His brain and his mouth did not seem to be working together. He sat down again.

There were a few titters from the class.

'It's all right, Roger.' Miss Runacres smiled knowingly. 'If you've got to go, you've got to go – that's fine – off you go.' She flapped a hand at him. 'Go on, Roger, go now.'

Roger rubbed his head again; he was feeling very uncomfortable. 'No, honestly, it's OK; I really don't need to go. I'm fine, I'll just sit here . . . carry on.'

There were a few gasps and more giggles.

'Oh, *thank you*, Roger,' said Miss Runacres, taking a deep breath. She had stopped smiling. 'If you're sure it's all right for me to . . . *carry on?*'

Roger's face was quite red as he nodded.

There was a lot more laughing.

'Now then, stop that,' said Miss Runacres, looking round the classroom. 'Settle down.' She gave Roger a grim look. 'So, *you're* happy for me to continue with the lesson?'

Roger immediately bounced to his feet, he knew *exactly* what he had to do, and stepped out from his desk. 'I want to go outside,' he bellowed, pointing at the door, *'now!'*

The classroom burst into loud laughter.

Miss Runacres gasped and stepped back. 'Roger Paxton!' she shouted over the noise. 'Stop this nonsense at once! Return to your seat immediately, or I'll take you to see Mrs Carmichael.'

'Oh, I'm sorry, Miss,' said Roger, lowering his arm and looking round sheepishly. 'I didn't mean that. I don't know why I said it.' He went back to his seat, sat down and stared at his desktop. *What's happening to me?*

'Quiet, children!' Miss Runacres held up both hands as the laughter continued.

'Please Miss, please Miss!' yelled Harry Caplan, sitting at the front beside the window.

'Quiet, children!' thundered Miss Runacres, and then she stamped her foot.

The classroom fell silent.

'That's . . . that's better.' Miss Runacres smoothed her skirt and glared at Roger. Her face was bright red.

'Now then—'

'Miss, Miss!' Harry Caplan waved frantically at the teacher.

'Not now, Harry!' snapped Miss Runacres.

Roger could feel something happening to him again. *A strange sensation.* He stood up. 'I've definitely *got* to go,' he said. The sensation faded, and he sat down again.

The children collapsed: Oliver Taylor started braying like a donkey, Aisha Shad fell off her chair and sat on the floor giggling hysterically, and Cameron Sharpe made *mumming* sounds as he rocked back and forth. The only pupil in the class *not* laughing was Harry Caplan. He continued to gaze out of the window with a look of utter joy on his face.

Miss Runacres put both hands over her bright red cheeks. She began taking sharp, short breaths.

'*Miss, Miss!*' Harry Caplan's high-pitched voice cut through the laughter.

Miss Runacres looked at Harry. '*What*? What is so important, Harry? *What* can't wait? Have I not got enough—'

Harry Caplan stood up.

'Not another one!' gasped Miss Runacres.

Harry pointed at the window beside the emergency door. 'Look there, Miss,' he said, a huge, happy smile on his face. 'There's an intergalactic, alien mega-being from outer space standing there. I think he's just landed and wants to come in!'

The entire classroom turned to look.

A dwarf was pressed up against the window – a ferocious-looking dwarf bristling with weapons and wearing a helmet. He had a wrinkly leathery face, covered in faint blue marks, a long grey beard, and he appeared to be about as broad as he was tall. And he looked as if he had just walked off the set of a fantasy film. The dwarf stepped back from the window and bowed. There was a large, two-headed axe strapped to his back.

Harry Caplan bowed back.

Miss Runacres began breathing faster; she made a noise like squeaking air escaping from a balloon as she hyperventilated.

The dwarf, still bowed over, suddenly charged forward and crashed through the window.

Miss Runacres collapsed in a dead faint.

'Invasion from outer space!' screamed Harry Caplan. 'They're not friendly! Run for it!'

The classroom erupted. Tables and chairs went flying as children fled towards the door. Within seconds the classroom was empty apart from Roger, still sitting at his desk, and Miss Runacres lying on the floor.

The dwarf marched over to Roger, shaking off the shards of glass from his shoulders and helmet.

'What are you doing here, Moss?' asked Roger, desperately trying to remain calm. 'Is that a new hat?'

Mossbelly MacFearsome rapped his knuckles on the helmet covering his head. 'It is not a *hat*, it is a battle-helmet!' He glanced down at Miss Runacres, grunted, and then looked round the classroom. 'Come,' he said to Roger, 'for we have no time to be wasted, we are once again to be boonfellows on a vital undertaking.'

'Actually, I'm going to stay with Maddie for a few days at the castle,' said Roger, drumming his fingers on the desk. 'My mum and dad said it was OK. So I can't go anywhere with you.'

'You are not going to the castle,' said Moss. 'The matter we have is grave and the time we have is—'

The school fire alarm started ringing.

'What *is* that infernal noise?' roared Moss, pulling out his sword. 'Have they loosed the bell-ringing bear from the Bass Rock?'

'It's the fire alarm,' yelled Roger, jumping to his feet, no longer feeling calm. 'Could you not have opened the door like a normal person?' He glared at Moss. 'Look at the mess you've made.'

Moss gave two loud sniffs. 'I smell no smoke and see no fire. The alarm is false.'

'It's for you!' screamed Roger, staring directly into Moss's face. 'Someone has pressed the fire alarm because of you!'

11

Moss looked down at himself. 'I am not on fire.'

'Oh you—' Roger stepped back. 'Did you do something to me just now? Something to my mind?'

'Not I,' said Moss. 'But Lady Goodroom was attempting to draw you out by using a command-spell. It did not work on your brain-head, your power of will must be too strong, so I came to get you as time is of the utmost importance.'

'Lady Goodroom's here?' shouted Roger over the deafening ringing.

'Yes,' he said impatiently. 'Come now, we must depart.'

'Is Maddie with her aunt?'

'She is,' nodded Moss.

'Oh. Well, just let me get my backpack and anorak.' Roger started towards the door, and then stopped. '*You*, stay here. Don't move; the cloakroom is just around the corner. I'll only be a second, OK?'

Without waiting for an answer Roger ran out of the classroom. The corridor outside was full of children running along in single file. Most of them were laughing excitedly. He pushed past the line of children and opened the first door on the right, unhooked his anorak from its peg and slipped it on. The zip stuck as he pulled it up.

There was a burst of yelling and shouting from the

corridor. Roger grabbed his backpack and flew out of the cloakroom – straight into Moss. It was like hitting a brick wall. He bounced off the dwarf and would have fallen over if Moss hadn't caught him. By now, the orderly line of children in the corridor had turned into a screaming mob fleeing in both directions.

'Come,' said Moss, shaking Roger by the shoulder, 'I have told you that we must hurry! We must capture or kill the Goblin Chief, Redcap, before the portal opens.'

'And *I* told you to wait where you were,' said Roger, pushing back at the dwarf and pointing at the now empty corridor. 'Now look what you've done.'

'I see nothing,' said Moss, looking up and down it.

'Exactly!' shouted Roger. 'You never see the trouble you cause.'

'No time for your idle chatter,' said Moss. 'We must leave.' He turned round and walked back to the classroom just as Miss Runacres came stumbling out of the door.

Moss stopped to let the teacher pass.

Miss Runacres gave Moss a groggy, lopsided smile. 'Thank you, young man,' she said. 'It's a lovely day.' She staggered past Roger without looking at him. 'I'm just going home to have a nice hot bath. Maybe a bit of cake to help with this noise ringing in my ears.'

'Look what you've done to that poor woman,' shouted

Roger, as his teacher slowly walked along the corridor mumbling to herself.

Moss shrugged. 'A touch feather-headed perhaps, but otherwise she has a pleasant disposition.'

Roger and Moss went back into the wrecked classroom and out through the broken window to the playing field at the side of the building. They started walking towards the school gates as children came pouring out of their classrooms and began lining up in rows in front of the school. The fire alarm was still ringing.

'What did you say we had to do?' shouted Roger. He had stopped in the middle of the playing field and was angrily pulling at the stuck zip on his anorak.

'Capture or kill the Goblin Chief, Redcap, before he opens the portal,' answered Moss. He pointed to a car at the school gates.

'You're crazy!' said Roger, as the zip came free at last. 'I'm not doing anything like that.'

'It is your blame that he was allowed to escape,' said Moss.

Roger stood, thinking for a moment. Behind him someone was shouting his name. Roger glanced back. Hugh Ball was running over.

'But then you lost track of him,' said Roger. 'You dwarves were going to find him. That's what you told us!'

'There is no time for you to fight with Hughumhughball,' said Moss, using his mistaken name for Hugh. He pulled out his sword. 'I'll dispatch him quickly.'

'No, no!' yelled Roger, holding up both hands at Moss, as Hugh Ball skidded to a halt in front of them. 'It's OK, Moss, we're not enemies any more, leave him alone.' He turned to Hugh. 'What do you want, Hugh?'

'Erm . . .' Hugh was staring at the sword in Moss's hand. 'I just wondered if you needed . . . any help?' He took a step backwards. 'That's . . . that's all. Just wondering . . .'

'No, thanks, Hugh,' said Roger. 'Um – this is my . . . my grandfather. Grandpa Moss . . . topher. He's come to collect me. We're going to a Halloween party.' He could see the look of shock on Hugh's face and couldn't help smiling to himself. 'He's a great fan of all that *Lord of the Rings* stuff; likes dressing up as them.' Roger raised his voice. 'Don't you, Grandpa Mosstopher?'

Moss just stared at Hugh. There was a ferocious expression on his face.

'Bit deaf,' said Roger.

'Oh, right.' Hugh licked his lips. 'Mosstopher? That's a very unusual name . . . He's very . . . It's a great costume . . . That sword looks so real . . . and sharp. Hope you have a nice . . . party.'

15

'You better go back, then,' said Roger. 'Thanks again, Hugh.'

Hugh Ball obediently turned and started running back towards the school building.

Moss muttered and sheathed his sword.

Roger could see the substantial figure of the head teacher, Mrs Carmichael, heading towards them as Hugh passed her going very fast in the other direction. 'OK, Moss,' said Roger, starting to run. 'Let's go.'

'Stop! Come back!' Mrs Carmichael shouted, wobbling dangerously on high heels.

Moss grunted and trotted after Roger.

'Don't get in that car,' screamed Mrs Carmichael, tottering along at her top speed.

The rear door of the car was open, and Lady Goodroom was hanging out of it waving her hands. Roger and Moss finally reached the Jaguar, climbed inside, and slammed the door behind them. As the car moved off, Roger turned to look out of the rear window.

The head teacher had stopped running; she was standing, gasping, with her hands on her hips, staring after them. There was a puzzled look on her face. Then she turned away, looked up at the sky, and scratched her head.

CHAPTER
Two

'All right, kiddo?' Wullie took one hand off the steering wheel, glanced in his rear-view mirror, and gave Roger a thumb's up. 'You're looking good, son. And now you're here, that's the gang all together again, eh?'

Roger smiled at the cheery face of the former delivery driver who had done so much to help them during the last adventure. 'I'm fine, Wullie,' he said, giving him a thumb's up back. 'Like your hat.'

'That's my chauffeur's hat I'm wearing today,' said Wullie, tapping his fingers on his grey, peaked cap. 'Smart innit?'

'Glad you joined us,' said Lady Goodroom, leaning over and grabbing Roger's head in both her hands. She planted a kiss on his forehead. 'Sorry about all the fuss, I was trying to send you a command-spell message but it didn't seem to work properly. Hope it didn't cause you any problems.' She looked at Moss. 'Someone who has no patience decided to go and get you himself.'

17

'And he just about wrecked the school and nearly killed my teacher,' said Roger, frowning at Lady Goodroom. He was wondering just how good her magic really was, as she was the one who had begun training him as an apprentice Warlockwatcher after the end of his last adventure.

There was a giggle from the other side of Lady Goodroom. 'Was that your teacher trying to get our registration number?' asked Maddie. 'She looked half-dead, puffing all over the place.'

'No, that was the head teacher, Mrs Carmichael,' said Roger. 'You should see the state of poor Miss Runacres.'

'Oh, dear,' said Lady Goodroom. 'That's a pity, poor woman. We'll need to see what we can do for her later.'

'If Mrs Carmichael got your registration she'll phone the police,' said Roger. 'She'll probably phone them anyway.'

'It should be all right,' said Lady Goodroom. 'I put a confusing-mind-spell on her. I'm pretty sure that it worked.'

'Better than the one you tried on me, I hope,' said Roger, before he could stop himself.

Maddie giggled and looked at her aunt.

'I've also got a back-up plan,' said Lady Goodroom, completely ignoring Roger's comment. 'And we've got a

18

lot to tell you. We are on a very dangerous mission, with very little time to fulfil it.'

Roger nodded. 'Something to do with Redcap, the Goblin Chief, Lady Goodroom.'

'Gwen,' said Lady Goodroom. 'I've told you to call me Gwen. And it's a lot more than—'

'I can do levitation now,' interrupted Maddie. 'Watch this.' She sat forward and wiggled all her fingers in the air. '*Flankenpop-blankenmix-zrifflegug*,' she said.

The cap on Wullie's head moved up slightly, hung in the air for a second, and then fell onto the seat beside him.

'*What the—?*' yelled Wullie. 'Stop that, ya mad wee Maddie! I could've crashed.'

'Maddie!' said Lady Goodroom, sternly. 'That's just silly. You could've tipped his hat over his eyes.'

'Oh, there was no danger,' said Maddie, as Wullie, one handed, picked up his hat and jammed it back on his head. 'I'm good at it.'

'No you're not,' said Lady Goodroom. 'You can raise some very small things a little way into the air. You need a lot more practice with all your spells.'

Maddie sat back, winked at Roger, and smiled innocently.

Roger grinned back at the sparkling hazel eyes and the lovely smile.

19

'Now, as I was saying,' said Lady Goodroom, giving Maddie a look, before turning to Moss. 'Have you told Roger about our problems?'

'A very little,' said Moss. 'He knows we must capture or destroy Redcap. What he doesn't know is, if we fail in our quest, the law states that the three of you will be incarcerated in Redcap's place under Dhùn Èideann Fort for the rest of *his* sentence! Which is at least a thousand years! And you'll all be dead when you are released!'

Roger's mouth dropped open, and he glanced at Maddie.

She nodded. She cupped a hand around her mouth and, in an exaggerated whisper, said: 'That's *Edinburgh Castle.*'

Roger grunted. 'I don't see what a goblin escaping from a prison has to do with us. We didn't know he was there. *Our* great quest was over! We'd smashed the Doomstone Sword and defeated Leatherhead Barnstorm and his gorefiends. It's not our fault there was a bit of leftover magic in the sword when we pushed it into the ground. We didn't know that! And it was just put there as a reminder of the trouble the human race would be in if they . . . *we* don't sort ourselves out. How were we supposed to know that where we stuck it was just above a . . . a *goblin*! And saying that we've to serve the rest of his sentence is daft. Doesn't make any sense.' He pointed at Moss. 'And anyway, it's rotten to lock someone up for a thousand years. *Even if it is a goblin*! That's terrible, no matter what they've done.'

'Too merciful,' said Moss. 'He should have been put to death. A thousand years is but the bite of a flea. Goblins are infernal things, evil creatures, with black hearts. They are not of this world. And it is your blame that he was allowed to escape.'

'What?' spluttered Roger. 'It was *you* dwarves who told us to put the Doomstone Sword in the ground there! *You* said it would be a good reminder that humans had only one hundred and thirty-seven years left to sort out the damage they're doing to themselves and the world – or else they would be destroyed by *dwarves* and . . . and *ogres!*'

'Your intentions do not matter,' said Moss. 'Dwarf law states that whomsoever frees a prisoner, shall recapture or kill the prisoner.' Moss smacked a fist against his hand. 'Or suffer the consequences!'

Roger opened his mouth to speak, thought better of it, and sat back with his arms folded.

Moss muttered and rumbled.

'What *is* the matter with you, anyway?' asked Roger, turning to Moss after a moment of silence. 'You're even grumpier than before.'

'I am not crumpsy,' said Moss, glowering at everyone. He pushed further back in his seat. 'I am carked.'

'I know, I know.' Lady Goodroom nodded, and silently mouthed *'worried'*. She smiled sympathetically. 'Listen, everyone. Captain Mossbelly has had his wedding postponed, so the sooner this is over with, the sooner he can get married.'

'Ach,' said Wullie. 'Sorry, wee man. I didn't know.'

'I'm sorry about that,' said Maddie.

Roger did not speak.

Lady Goodroom cleared her throat, and then did it again.

Roger sighed. 'Fine. I'm sorry that's happened, Moss. But I still don't see why we should have to—'

'"*See*"!' roared Moss, twisting to face Roger. 'You'll see nothing when you're rotting in a prison, and the world above you is destroyed, you hoddypeak!'

Roger flinched at the angry face spitting at him. 'All right, all right, take it easy. What are you on about? Destroying the world? I thought this was about capturing a goblin. And how could a goblin destroy the world?'

'I have previously told you this,' said Moss, banging his fists together. 'You have released a monster! If we do not stop him he will open the portal.' Moss took a deep breath and sat back in his seat. 'The goblins will again invade earth. There will be war, great bloodshed.'

'*I* didn't release him?' Roger shouted back, and shook his head. He looked at Lady Goodroom. 'And it can't be worse than last time.'

'Nothing like last time,' growled Moss. 'Leatherhead Barnstorm was a rutterkin leading a band of whifflings. *This* is an invasion from another dimension! Goblins, the most detestable of all creatures! Dwarves hate goblins.'

'I think we got that,' said Roger, still looking at Lady Goodroom. 'So who is Redcap anyway? And how can he even be here, if he's from another dimension?'

'I'm telling you now,' spluttered Moss. 'Your ears are stuffed with hairy caterpillars and your—'

Lady Goodroom stretched forward and patted Moss's knee. 'Let me explain, Captain. Might be easier if I tell him. You can set me right if I get anything wrong.' She continued to pat him on the knee.

Moss *hurrumphed*, stroked his beard, and then gave a brief nod.

'Good,' said Lady Goodroom, sitting back. She looked at Roger. 'Unfortunately Redcap was not recaptured, and we are the only ones who can stop the horror from being unleashed.' She took a breath. 'And there's so little time left.'

CHAPTER
Three

'A long while ago, nearly eight hundred years,' said Lady
Goodroom, as the car sped along the road to Edinburgh,
'near the village of Gifford in East Lothian lived a
powerful warlock, a so-called necromancer. He was Sir
Hugo de Gifford, known as the Wizard of Yester Castle,
and he created a key, in the shape of a dodecahedron, to
open an interdimensional door . . . to another world.' She
pointed at Moss. 'The dwarves refer to it as a portal. Well,
Sir Hugo opened it and unleashed a fearful goblin
army, under his command, to conquer our world. The
monstrous goblin chief, Redcap, led them, and there was
a terrible war. But the dwarves and their allies defeated
the goblins at the great battles of Cowlairs and
Cowcaddens, and Redcap was captured and imprisoned,
for ever, under Edinburgh Castle.'

'Why was he put in prison, *for ever*?' asked Maddie.
'That's a bit much.'

'He was the only one who knew the exact location of

24

the portal, but he refused to say where it was,' said Lady Goodroom. She looked at Moss for confirmation. 'If he'd told them the location, his sentence would not have been so severe. As I understand it, dwarf wizards placed him in a state of suspended animation?'

Moss nodded. 'If he had disclosed the whereabouts of the portal, then he would have only been confined for one thousand years.'

'Time off for good behaviour, then,' said Wullie, laughing.

'Did the humans not fight the goblins?' asked Roger.

'No,' said Lady Goodroom. 'They were under goblin mind-control and couldn't help. It's *one* of the reasons that, after it was all over, the dwarves started using trusted human Witchwatchers to keep an eye on what was happening above ground.'

Moss made a loud snorting noise. 'The humans faffled about like pigs without bottoms; they thought they were fighting Norway! Ran about shouting and tripping over their feet. Useless.'

'No one found the portal, then?' Roger asked Lady Goodroom.

'No,' said Lady Goodroom. 'There was nothing for them to find. It was gone. They searched and searched, but you can't find something that's just not there any more.' She looked at Moss, who shook his head.

Lady Goodroom continued. 'After the battles, Yester Castle was destroyed as the dwarves searched for the opening to the portal. Just some bits of it were left standing. And the steps to the lower dungeons were eventually blocked off because, as time passed, legends began to emerge that it was a passage to hell where demons lived.'

'What happened to the man who opened the porthole?' asked Roger.

Maddie giggled. Moss grunted and rolled his eyes.

'*Portal*,' said Lady Goodroom, gently. She smiled at Roger. 'Sir Hugo was never seen again; must have been slain in one of the battles.'

'So what's all the panic about?' asked Roger. 'Why've we got so little time?' He leaned forward. 'I know we've got to capture Redcap . . . but why the sudden rush?'

'The portal is about to open,' said Lady Goodroom. 'Redcap is going to unleash the goblins, again.'

'How?' asked Roger. 'How can he do that?'

'He has the dodecahedron,' rumbled Moss, 'the key to the portal.'

'You said that word earlier.' Roger looked at Moss. 'What *is* a doh-deca-thing?'

'You don't know what a dodecahedron is?' Maddie laughed. 'What a silly boy you are.'

Lady Goodroom flapped a hand at Maddie. 'Stop that, Maddie, *you* didn't know.' She turned to Roger and held out her hand with her fingers curled upwards. 'Think of it as a solid, round object with twelve flat sides. Got it?'

Roger looked puzzled. He raised his eyes as he tried to imagine it and shrugged. 'OK, what does it do?'

'When placed in the correct spot,' Moss pointed at Lady Goodroom's hand, 'and with the correct incantations, it turns like a key to open the portal.'

Lady Goodroom nodded solemnly, and dropped her hand onto her lap. 'And once it's open, the goblins will pour through.'

There were a few moments of silence in the car.

'But . . .' began Roger, then he stopped and thought again. 'How do you know he's got this doh-doh key? Did he have it with him when he was in prison under Edinburgh Castle? That would have been really stupid to leave it with him.'

'No, no.' Lady Goodroom shook her head, wobbling her chins. 'After the great battle of Cowcaddens, it was found by dwarves and given to us humans as a reminder of the goblin invasion.'

'As a reminder of their stupidity!' bellowed Moss.

'It was in the Kelvingrove Museum in Glasgow,' Lady Goodroom continued. 'They had it wrongly labelled as a Roman artefact. It was stolen a few weeks ago. There was a bit in the paper about it.'

'Oh,' said Roger. He shook his head. 'Didn't know.'

Moss sighed.

'No harm could come of the dodecahedron being in the humans' possession – as long as Redcap remained imprisoned!'

'You should have smashed it,' shouted Wullie from the driver's seat. 'Then you'd be laughing.'

'There is no jocularity in this, Wullie,' Moss shouted back.

'I didnae mean that kind of laughing, son,' said Wullie, talking to his rear-view mirror.

'How do you know Redcap has it?' asked Roger. 'Might not be him who took it.'

'Because,' said Lady Goodroom, 'it was stolen by two security guards. And when they were questioned afterwards, they each said that they were persuaded to do it by a small man who convinced them that it belonged to his family and they would be handsomely rewarded.'

Moss snorted.

'And both swear,' continued Lady Goodroom, 'that when they gave it to the small man, he immediately changed into a fiendish-looking goblin and ran away, cackling.' She lifted a folded newspaper. 'And look at this. This is an article in yesterday's paper about strange goings-on at Yester Castle.' She passed the newspaper to Roger.

Roger quickly read the slightly humorous piece about reports of shrieking and revelry coming from the ruins. The report said that it was either the ghost of Sir Hugo or, more likely, local youths out enjoying themselves.

'And you think this is . . .?' Roger handed the paper back to Lady Goodroom just as Wullie pulled into a layby and came to a stop.

'We are fairly sure that it is him,' said Lady Goodroom. She reached out to the car door-handle. 'And we think that he has already placed the dodecahedron key to open the portal.'

Roger thought again. 'Well, why hasn't it opened then?'

'The portal can only open, at midnight, on one special day each year,' said Lady Goodroom. 'The day Sir Hugo cast the spells.'

'When is that?' asked Roger.

'All Hallows' Eve!' Moss almost spat the words out.

Roger looked round at the others in the car. 'When is . . . what's that?'

'Halloween, silly!' shouted Maddie.

'Oh,' said Roger, 'so it is.' His eyes widened. 'But that's tonight.'

'Exactly!' Lady Goodroom opened the car door. 'We've got hardly any time left before the portal opens and goblins invade the world.'

CHAPTER
Four

As Roger climbed out of the car he was surprised to see Lord Goodroom leaning against a slightly battered van.

'Bang on time,' shouted Lord Goodroom, walking over to his wife. 'No problems, me dear?' he asked in his clipped English accent and handed her two sets of keys and a piece of paper.

'A little, Pen,' answered Lady Goodroom, giving him a quick hug, 'nothing to worry about, though. Petrol in the van?'

'Nearly full,' said Lord Goodroom, as Wullie handed him the key to the Jaguar. He pointed at the paper his wife was holding. 'That's the address of the cottage I've hired and the keys to get in. And I've put in some grub in case you don't have time to get anything. The torches are in the glove-box.'

'Well done,' said Lady Goodroom. 'Be careful now, don't do anything silly. If they try to stop you, just pull over immediately.'

31

'Don't worry, I know what to do,' said Lord Goodroom, opening the car door. 'I go from here to the airport car park, and leave this there. Then I hire a car from the airport to take me home, and I wait at home until I hear from you. I'll be fine.' He smiled at Roger. 'It's very nice to see you again, my boy.' Lord Goodroom waved as he slid into the driver's seat. 'Good luck everybody!'

Roger raised a hand in a half-hearted wave. 'Nice to see—'

'I'll phone you,' yelled Lady Goodroom, as the driver's door clunked shut. 'And don't drive too fast!'

A moment later the Jaguar shot out of the layby and roared off up the road.

'What was all that?' asked Roger, as the car disappeared. 'He didn't even—'

'No time just now,' said Lady Goodroom. 'Hurry, hurry. Tell you when we're on our way again, everyone in.' She threw keys to Wullie, and then slid the van's side-door open. 'Hurry!'

There were two bench seats in the back of the van. Roger and Maddie sat in the rear with Lady Goodroom and Moss in front of them.

'Buckle-up,' said Wullie, starting the engine. 'Next stop—' He swivelled around in his seat and looked at

32

Lady Goodroom. 'Where are we going again, yer Lady Mamship?'

'Yester Castle, near the village of Gifford,' said Lady Goodroom, looking at the piece of paper in her hand. 'Just drive to Edinburgh, take the ring road, then I'll give you directions.' She turned round in her seat and looked back at Roger. 'This is a safer vehicle for us to use, just in case anyone saw you leaving in the middle of all that mayhem.'

Roger nodded. 'OK.' He leaned forward a little. 'How do you know the goblins will come through this . . . portal? What you told me happened hundreds of years ago; they might have changed since then. Even Redcap might have changed.'

'Don't speak such fadoodle,' bellowed Moss, bouncing up and down in his seat, 'you poop-noddy! He is *Redcap* the Goblin Chief. He is named that because he dips his hat in his victims' blood! This is a fiend! Some of your olden-day people thought they were being visited by *demons*!'

'OK, OK!' shouted Roger at the back of Moss's head. 'I'm only saying. He might just be trying to go home. He *might* have changed.'

There was a growling-rumbling noise from Moss. Lady Goodroom put her hand on the dwarf's arm and

33

gave it a gentle squeeze. 'Roger,' she said, turning her head a little, but not enough to look at him, 'this is a vicious killer we are talking about. He's been in suspended animation for hundreds of years, so he'll be exactly the same as when he was captured.'

'OK,' said Roger. 'What's the plan?'

'Well, we know Redcap is near Yester Castle or the village of Gifford,' said Lady Goodroom. 'So we'll go to the castle first, search it, and if we don't have any luck, then we'll go to the village and try there.' She leaned her head back and spoke a little softer. 'But the dwarves have a tracker in the area who apparently knows where Redcap is. So we're hoping the tracker contacts us. Isn't that right, Captain?'

'Indeed true,' said Moss. 'A fine dwarf, Bloodbone Knottenbelt, has sent knowledge of Redcap's whereabouts. And, although he has not been heard from for some days, I am confident he will make contact with us when we arrive at the castle.' He paused for a moment. 'Unless . . .'

Lady Goodroom squeezed Moss's arm again. 'I'm sure he's fine. In the meantime why don't you tell us all about goblins. What we should be looking out for. How best to identify one.'

'Goblins!' Moss roared the word out and started to shake with fury. 'They are creatures from a hellish place!

34

They kill without mercy. They eat anything – including their babies if they are hungry! What more do you need to know? They are goblins!'

'Calm down, Captain,' said Lady Goodroom, in a soothing voice. 'Just tell us what you know. You are the only one here with any knowledge of the goblins.'

'*I* only know what I've read on ancient writing pages, and been told by dwarf whitebeards,' answered Moss, in a slightly calmer voice. 'I had not been delivered to the world when the great battles were fought.'

'That's fine,' said Lady Goodroom. 'Whatever you know will help.'

'Well . . .' began Moss. 'Goblins are terrified of writing – they draw pictures instead. They hate the cold for their own world is hot, very hot. And their greed is so great that they will eat anything, but especially salty or pickled food. They would gorge all day on salty-pickly things, for they cannot get enough of it. They also fear horses and dogs, and love gold and jewellery; they covet dwarf gold.'

'I see,' said Lady Goodroom, nodding slowly. 'That's useful. And how might we know Redcap himself? What should we be looking for?'

'It is a difficult task,' said Moss. 'He will have used his ability to manipulate minds, he will appear to be what he is not.'

'How does he do that?' asked Maddie.

Moss thought for a moment. 'He has a power to delve into the simple, subconscious minds of humans. Mind-melding. He creates a picture-image that is not a true picture-image. It is only a picture-image that he shows, creating a picture-image of what is not there. It is a *false* picture-image.' Moss held up his hands. 'Do you understand the meaning of my words?'

'Does he create a picture-image?' asked Maddie, stroking her chin in an exaggerated manner.

'You have it, Mad-one,' said Moss, nodding solemnly.

Wullie hunched over the steering wheel, his shoulders shaking with laughter.

'Then I ask you again, *how* will we find him?' asked Lady Goodroom, with slight irritation in her voice. 'There must be some way to identify him.'

'Mmmmm,' said Moss, and he mumbled to himself. 'Let me use my brain-memory for remembrance.' He gazed upwards. 'Yes,' he said, 'my remembrance is good. I have brought into my brain-memory two things that will help our quest.' He folded his arms over his chest.

'Well?' Lady Goodroom sighed. 'What are they?'

'Do you know what happens when you place a bread-crust on a fork and hold it over a roasting fire for too long, and it burns?' Moss continued speaking without waiting for an answer, 'You know the stenching it creates?'

'Yes,' said Lady Goodroom. 'Not a pleasant smell.'

'Then that is what we must sniff,' said Moss. 'He will smell of it.'

'He smells like burnt toast?' Lady Goodroom sounded puzzled.

Moss nodded. 'All goblins are foul-smelling like that. Their blood is oily and sizzles round their bodies like hot fat, singeing off all body hair.' He stroked his beard. 'They cannot stand our magnificent whiskers. And the recorded writings stated that as Chief Goblin, Redcap's pungent aroma was worse than any other of the vile creatures.'

Maddie leaned forward and tapped Moss on the shoulder. 'What's the other thing we've to look out for?'

'Ah, yes.' Moss turned slightly, trying to look at Maddie. 'The other certain sign of a goblin is that they fart into bottles to make their drinks fizzy.'

There was a second's silence and then everyone, with the exception of Moss, burst into laughter. Wullie almost lost control of the van, swerving dangerously for a few moments. There were several angry *honks* from other motorists.

'*What ails you?*' Moss looked round in amazement at

his companions as they tried to control their giggles. 'I have told you the two certain ways of identifying Redcap – and you guffaw like feather-heads!'

'Sorry, Captain,' said Lady Goodroom, dabbing her eyes with a handkerchief. 'No offence intended, I'm sure. It's just that . . .' she started laughing again, 'you paint such a wonderful image.'

'You sure do, Mossy,' yelled Wullie from his driver's seat. 'We've to look out for someone who smells like burnt toast and does fizzy farts – shouldn't be too difficult to find!'

CHAPTER
Five

There was a light drizzle of rain falling as Roger and the gang began the difficult journey along the path to Yester Castle. Moss was leading the way, with Roger and Maddie following and Wullie, helping Lady Goodroom, bringing up the rear.

They had parked the van close to a large wooded area before setting off, and were now on the steep trail leading up to the ruins. It was hard going; they stumbled over tree roots and broken branches and they slipped on rotted ferns and wet leaves. No one spoke as they struggled to keep up with the person in front of them. The only one who was moving easily was Moss. He would stop every so often and wait impatiently until the others caught up with him.

As the path began to level out, Roger could hear a roaring noise coming from far below. Looking down, he could see a river at the bottom of a sheer gorge.

'Do not look at that downsteepy.' Moss spoke without stopping or looking back. 'A tumble there would be death.'

Roger fixed his eyes on the broad bottom in front of him and wondered how Moss knew where he had been looking.

Moss rounded a bend and stopped. 'Look there,' he said, pointing.

Roger could just see a slender piece of stone wall poking through the trees.

'Is that the castle?' Maddie's voice was quiet.

'It is.' Moss slowly slid his sword out of its scabbard. 'Keep close.'

As they moved forward again, the walls of a ruined castle gradually appeared out of a thin mist. There was an eerie silence: nothing rustled, nothing moved.

Moss held up his hand, signalling everyone to stop.

'Listen carefully for a reply to my realistic imitation of an owl-bird,' said Moss. He gently slid the tip of his sword into the ground, and then cupped both hands over his mouth.

'*Tiwit-tiwoo, tiwit-tiwoo.*'

There was silence.

'*Tiwit-tiwoo, tiwit-tiwoo.*'

Silence.

'Bloodbone is not answering,' said Moss, grasping his sword again. 'Now, we search the castle.'

'Are you sure this is a good idea, Mossyman?' asked Wullie, glancing about. 'It's getting dark out here and anything could be hiding in there.'

'It is not a *good* idea,' said Moss, stopping in front of the ruin. 'But it is the only idea I have in my possession.' He pointed his sword at a half-arched doorway partly buried in the ground. 'We enter there.'

'Through that!' said Lady Goodroom. 'Don't think I'll manage through that, it looks a bit too tight for me.'

'You remain here,' said Moss, 'if Redcap is not within the castle, then we must have protection to guard our backs. I'll enter with one of the younghedes.'

'They would be safer outside with me,' said Lady Goodroom, leaning against a broken tree-stump.

'At least one of you must be present when Redcap is captured or slain,' said Moss. 'To fulfil the law it must be that way. I'll take the Destroyer.' He handed Roger a dagger.

'I'll go as well,' said Maddie.

'Aye, me too.' Wullie stepped forward. 'Give me one of yer weapons.'

'You must remain here!' Moss spoke sharply. 'There may be close combat in a confined and darkened space.

41

Too many of us and we'll be fighting ourselves.' He handed his battle-axe to Wullie and his cudgel to Lady Goodroom. 'I have made my decision. Stay by the entrance and if you do not hear my voice – kill whatever comes out.'

'But . . .' Wullie shook the axe he was holding. 'I can—'

'Butter me no buts!' Moss pointed his sword at Wullie. 'You have my commands. Obey!' He turned to Roger. 'We go!'

Roger looked at the archway and gulped. He took a small step and stopped. He had a familiar feeling creeping over him – he was scared.

'Oh, Captain . . .' said Lady Goodroom, softly.

'By the thundering burps of Stickleback Stillabed, what is it now?' Moss spun round.

'It's nearly dark out here,' said Lady Goodroom, pulling two small torches out of a pocket. 'And it'll be much worse in there. These might help you to see.'

Moss grunted and took both torches. He handed one to Roger, and then *clicked* the one he was holding on and off several times. 'Good,' he said, with the torch switched on. 'Light-beams will make our task easier. I do not have any fire-making equipment with me, so you should have given me this information earlier.' He looked at Roger. 'Do you know how to operate a light beam?'

42

Roger just nodded and clicked his torch on and off.

'That is correct,' said Moss. 'Then, together, we step forward into the unknown.'

Moss strode forward, shoulders back, and head erect. There was a loud *boing!* as his helmet hit the top of the arch. He staggered a little, then ducked quickly and passed through.

Muffled laughter followed Roger as he ducked under the archway. He wasn't feeling too good; his stomach was churning, and only one thought kept running through his mind as he followed Moss – *why is it always me?*

CHAPTER
Six

Roger crept along, his torch playing over the dripping stones in the narrow passage. Moss was well in front of him now, and his torchlight had just come to a halt.

'This is Goblin Hall,' said Moss, as Roger caught up. The dwarf was shining his light over the floor of a large chamber. 'Keep your wink-a-peeps watchful for a goblin leaping out at you.'

Roger played his torch beam on the walls and curved ceiling. He was standing at one end of the chamber; chunks of masonry and rubbish covered the floor. On the far wall were two unevenly spaced iron-grated windows, and from the upper window a single ray of moonlight penetrated the darkness. There was a dank, rotting smell with a slight burnt-toast aroma lurking in the background. Roger was starting to sweat and, at the same time, a cold chill was creeping over him. He was terrified of this place.

'It's empty,' said Roger, trying to control the panic building within him. 'Please, can we go back now?'

Moss sniffed. 'Can you not smell that bread-burning stench?' He sniffed again. 'He has been here, recently. Or perhaps he still lurks within.'

Roger tried to sniff again, but he was having difficulty just breathing, and his teeth were beginning to chatter. 'C-can we just go?'

'Look there!' said Moss, the beam from his torch shining in the far corner of the dark chamber. 'See!'

'Wh-what?' Roger could barely speak.

'Use your wink-a-peeps, boy.' Moss strode across the floor and stood looking into the corner.

Roger scuttled after him and shone his shaking torch in the same direction. He could see roughly-hewn steps cut into the floor. Moss stood above the steps and bellowed: 'Come out, foul creature! Come and fight like a dwarf, you whiffling!'

There was silence, apart from the ringing in Roger's ears.

'L-look there!' Roger waggled his torch at the corner just above the steps. 'What's all that? Looks like . . . looks like *little bones*.'

Moss kneeled down and picked through the small pile of white things on the damp floor. He stood up and growled.

'What?' Roger shone his torch in Moss's face. 'Why are you growling? Tell me! What's wrong?'

45

'They are the remains of a small animal,' said Moss, his face ghastly in the torchlight. 'I fear that they could be the bones from a water vole.'

'A water vole—?'

'Be quiet!' thundered Moss. 'Shine your light down there, keep it steadfast, don't move . . . and . . .'

'And what?' Roger held the torch in both hands to keep it steady.

Moss began – slowly – descending the steps.

'And what?' hissed Roger.

'Be ready to flee,' came Moss's voice, as he turned a corner and vanished into darkness.

Roger stood, quaking. He tried to hold his torch steady but it was very difficult. The inky darkness was closing in and, worse, he was certain that he could hear *something* crawling along the floor behind him. *It was Redcap.* He was sure of it. He desperately wanted to turn and see, but if he did, he would see what it was! Roger trembled. *Moss had been down there for ages. Perhaps he wasn't coming back! Maybe he'd been— What? Time to turn and run! That was the only sensible thing to do. Moss would have been back by now if he was still—*

There was a scraping noise from below.

Roger's torchlight was dancing about, and he was sweating even harder. He could feel it running down his back. *Or perhaps it wasn't sweat – it might be something crawling . . .*

A light appeared, followed by Moss's head.

Roger nearly melted with relief.

The dwarf came up slowly, his boots scraping on the rough steps. He stood beside Roger and spoke quietly. 'We leave here now, Roger. The foul creature is not down there, and further on is blocked with rocks. There is neither goblin nor portal in this vile place.'

'OK,' said Roger, trying not to sound too desperate. He turned and quickly shone his torch over the walls and floor. *There was nothing there!* 'I'll go first, this time,' he said, almost running across the floor of the chamber.

'Remember to speak who you are!' Moss shouted after him.

'It's me, me, me!' Roger bawled at the top of his voice as he tore along the passage. 'Coming out, coming out!'

He burst out into a moonlit night and stood breathing in huge gulps of air as Lady Goodroom, Maddie and Wullie gathered round. Moments later Moss came out of the archway and stood at the entrance with his head bowed.

'What happened? Did you find the portal?' Lady Goodroom and Wullie spoke at once.

'Did you kill Redcap?' asked Maddie.

Roger was having difficulty finding his voice. His skin was rapidly cooling in the night air.

'He was not there, Mad-one,' said Moss. He spoke quietly, a slight tremor in his voice, and stared at the ground. 'Nor was there any sign of a portal. We have to search elsewhere.'

'Why did you think that the white things were the bones from a vole?' asked Roger, handing back the dagger. He was beginning to feel a little better now that he was out of that horrible place.

Moss switched off his torch and gave it to Lady Goodroom before answering. 'When we are forced to send dwarves to the Upperworld, we use voles to carry our messages. It is our method of communicating. Sometimes we use toads, but they are not as reliable. They lack the concentration, and tend to jump into every pond they meet, or are too slow crossing where the combustion carriages travel . . . and do not arrive at their destination, ever.' Moss paused and looked round at the faces bathed in moonlight. 'That was Bloodbone Knottenbelt's message-vole in there – or rather, its bones.'

'How could it be its bones?' asked Wullie. 'That canny be . . . unless . . .'

'The goblin devoured it,' said Moss. 'Picked it clean.'

'Eaten it?' Maddie had a disgusted look. 'You're joking!'

'There is no jocularity in my voice,' said Moss.

'I don't think that I'd fancy that for—' Wullie stopped talking and looked down.

'Then where is your tracker, Bloodbone Knottenbelt?' Lady Goodroom's voice was a little shaky as she asked her question. 'And how can you tell from just the vole's bones that it was Bloodbone's?'

'Because *his* bones are at the bottom of the stairs,' said Moss, in a throaty voice. 'They were left there for us to find.'

CHAPTER
Seven

'I feel sick,' said Maddie. 'That's the most horrible thing I've ever heard of in my life.'

'Are you sure, son?' Wullie handed back Moss's battle-axe.

'Go and see for yourself, Wullie,' said Moss. 'His bones are beside his helmet.'

'No, no, yer all right, I'll take your word.'

'What now, Captain?' asked Lady Goodroom, quietly. 'What are your thoughts?'

Moss cleared his throat. 'Bloodbone Knottenbelt was one of my friendship companions. He was a straight-fingered fellow, and many a tankard of merry-go-down we supped together over a shared baccy-pouch. He was a boonfellow with a hearty laugh. I'll miss him.' He stroked his beard. 'Those are my thinking-thoughts at this time, Lady Goodroom.'

'No, I meant what do you think we should do now?' asked Lady Goodroom.

'Ah,' said Moss. 'I was in another place.' He raised his head and breathed deeply. 'Well now, I have only brain-thoughts for the whiteliver, Redcap, but, alas, none for finding him, or the portal. I was certain-sure that Bloodbone would help us find Redcap . . .' He sighed and shrugged his shoulders. 'We could try the location of Gifford village.'

'But what would we do there?' asked Maddie. 'Go round all the houses knocking on the doors and asking them if they're really a goblin?'

'Well . . .' said Roger, slowly, 'that's not such a bad idea! It *is* the one night of the year when you can knock on people's doors: Halloween! We might get lucky.'

There was silence for a few moments.

'Ehm,' said Wullie, 'I'm with Roger. Think about it for a minute. Half the people will be out enjoying themselves, while the other half will be at home handing out sweets.' He pointed at Roger and Maddie. 'These two could go round the doors, guising! You know, what's it called now, tricky-treating.'

'We would certainly have access to a lot more people,' said Lady Goodroom. She looked at Moss and then glanced at her watch. 'What do you think, Captain? We're running out of time.'

51

'We have nothing else,' said Moss. 'Let us go and do this tricky-treating.'

Roger and the gang were silent on their way down the hill from Yester Castle, and the path was even more treacherous. Lady Goodroom had to be helped several times as she slipped and stumbled, and on one occasion landed with a loud *thump* on her bottom.

When they reached level ground, Maddie was the first to break the silence.

'I was actually really glad I didn't have to go in that terrible castle.' Maddie took hold of Roger's arm as she whispered to him. 'What was it *like*?'

'Awful,' said Roger. He shuddered. 'It was the worst thing I've ever done. I hated it.'

'You were *very* brave,' said Maddie, giving his arm a squeeze and then suddenly letting go. She had stopped walking.

'I *was* very scared,' said Roger, feeling quite pleased at the attention. 'But I just felt as if I had to—'

'Shush!' said Maddie. 'Stop talking. What was that noise? Did you hear that?'

Everyone stopped.

'I hear nothing but the wind,' said Moss.

'A forest creature?' Lady Goodroom rubbed at her bottom and winced.

Maddie shook her head. 'It sounded like a *scream*.'

Everyone listened. The wind was moaning softy, some leaves rustled along the path.

Roger opened his mouth to speak – then he heard it: three faint sounds, one after another, hardly a space between them.

'There!' said Maddie. 'That was it! Three screams this time.' She looked round. 'You must have heard them.'

'I heard them,' said Roger, as the others shook their heads. 'But I don't think they're screams. They sounded more like sneezes to me.'

'Yer both hearing things,' said Wullie. 'I never heard nothing!'

'Younghedes' lug-holes are better than ours,' said Moss. 'We should investigate.'

'Over there,' said Maddie pointing to her left.

'Yes, that was where I heard it coming from,' said Roger.

'Come,' said Moss. 'Bring light-beams again, it is dark in there.' He pulled out his sword and stepped off the path into the forest. 'Let us find the source of the screaming-sneezes.'

Moss led the gang through the forest until the trees began to thin out and Roger could just see a bright moon shining in a now cloudless night sky.

'There,' hissed Moss, stopping. He switched off his torch.

Roger and the others didn't speak; they could plainly see the frightful sight in front of them.

They were gathered beyond the last trees of the forest. Below them was a long stretch of meadowland leading downhill to a meandering stream. On the other side of the stream a golf flag fluttered in the breeze. Near where they were standing was a small rock-face jutting out from the hill, and silhouetted against the rock-face were two shadowy, misshapen figures.

'Two of them,' said Wullie, quietly. 'That's no right. Do you think he's got a goblin pal?'

'Looks more like two *monsters* to me,' whispered Maddie.

'They are strange-looking,' said Lady Goodroom, still trying to catch her breath after the walk through the forest. 'Let's just wait a bit and see what they are.'

'No time for waiting,' said Moss, sheathing his sword and pulling out his battle-axe. 'We charge now.'

'Aaaatishooo! Aaaatishooo!'

'That's definitely sneezing,' said Lady Goodroom. 'Do goblins sneeze?'

Suddenly the rock-face began to glow a deep blue colour. '*What's that?*' gasped Roger. It pulsed brighter, and then slowly faded out again.

'The portal!' shouted Maddie, jumping up and down. 'We've found it!' Then she stopped. '*Ooops!* Shouldn't have said that out loud.'

The shadowy figures moved away from the rock-face and turned towards the gang. One of the figures was a glistening yellow colour and was grasping a huge round axe-thing. The other figure, standing further back in the shadows, had no visible weapon. The yellow figure shook its weapon several times – and then sneezed.

'They're sneezing *monsters!*' yelled Maddie.

'*King Golmar's braces!*' roared Moss, and he began running with his battle-axe raised above his head. '*For Bloodbone Knottenbelt!*'

Roger and the others looked at each other for a second, and then started running after him. Lady Goodroom tripped almost immediately. Roger and Maddie stopped to help her.

'Go on! Go on!' Lady Goodroom struggled to her feet, brushing her skirt. 'I'll catch up. Go on!'

'Wait for me, wee man,' screamed Wullie. 'I'm right behind you – and gies one o' yer weapons.'

'*Kirkiemachough*, you white-livered rutterkins!' bellowed Moss, running faster.

Both shadowy figures stood facing the charging dwarf. The yellow figure raised its axe and began to advance. Moss bounced forward and swung his battle-axe in both hands. The blade *hummed* through the air, cutting through the shaft of the round axe, and slicing off the top of the yellow figure's head.

As the yellow figure collapsed, Moss crouched down ready for the second figure as it stepped forward. It looked at Moss and said sternly: 'You're in a lot of trouble for that. I'm going to write you a ticket.'

CHAPTER
Eight

Roger and Maddie arrived just behind Wullie. They stood, panting, watching as a traffic warden slapped a ticket on Moss's chest.

Moss, his battle-axe still held ready to strike, lowered his chin and looked down. The ticket fell off his chest and fluttered away.

'I'll just give you another one,' said the traffic warden. 'Don't think you're getting away with it, because you're not.'

Moss lowered his battle-axe. The traffic warden ripped off the fresh ticket and held it out. 'Take it,' he said. 'Go on! You can't go around destroying council property, you know. Oh, no. That lollipop pole you broke belongs to the council.' He nodded at the figure on the ground. 'Alf belongs to the council. So do I.' He waved the ticket at Moss. 'Here, take this if you don't want any more trouble.'

Moss stretched out his hand and took the ticket just

57

as Lady Goodroom arrived. She kneeled down beside the elderly lollipop man in his yellow coat.

'Is he dead?' asked Wullie.

'No,' said Lady Goodroom, indicating the peaked hat lying on the ground. 'Just knocked his hat off. He was lucky.'

The lollipop man sat up and sneezed. 'This cold's getting worse,' he said, putting a hand on top of his head and looking round. 'Where's my bunnet gone?'

'What are they?' Moss glared at the lollipop man and the traffic warden. 'They wear uniforms,' he pointed at the lollipop man, 'but this one is not a warrior. He is an old human. He must have attained at least a hundred years in human life.'

'Hey, you,' said the lollipop man, getting to his feet with help from Lady Goodroom and Wullie. Roger handed him his hat. 'Watch yer cheek or I'll fetch you a belt across the ear. I'm no a day past seventy.' He put on his hat, pulled it down tightly, and looked over at the traffic warden. 'Come on, John,' he pointed at the rock-face, 'we'd better get back to guarding that thing again. Now . . . where did I put my lollipop pole?'

Alf and John took up their positions in front of the rock-face; John holding his ticket machine, and Alf clutching the top part of his broken lollipop sign.

'What *are* you?' thundered Moss, hefting his axe and stepping towards Alf and John. 'Tell me or I'll let your brains out of your heads.'

John held up his ticket machine. 'I'm warning you, any closer and you'll get another one.'

'Halt,' said Alf, waving his broken sign. 'No crossing until safe to do so.'

Moss rumbled like a small volcano.

'Leave them alone,' said Lady Goodroom, stepping in front of Moss. 'They are under a mind-control. I'll deal with them.' She looked closely at the two men. 'Who sent you here?' she asked, speaking loudly. She leaned even closer. 'Can you tell us where we can find the person who sent you?'

'Away and bile yer heid you auld bam-pot,' said Alf, equally loudly, and then he sneezed all over Lady Goodroom.

'Leave this tae me, Ladymam,' said Wullie, pushing Lady Goodroom to one side. 'This is like a hypnotism type mind-control thing they're in, isn't it? What we were talking about before?'

'I suppose, yes,' said Lady Goodroom, wiping her face.

'Right then,' said Wullie, 'give us your torch, and watch closely, see what an expert can do. Someone who knows what they're talking about.'

Lady Goodroom handed a torch to Wullie who switched it on and held it under his chin. He stepped closer and bent into John's face.

'Look into my eyes,' said Wullie, in a strange voice. 'Look into my eyes, deep into my eyes, just my eyes, my eyes, my eyes.'

John craned forward and locked eyes with Wullie. They both stared hard at each other for a few moments, and then Wullie slowly raised his right hand . . . and snapped his fingers!

John blinked several times, shook his head, and looked round. 'Where am I? What am I doing out here? Who are you people?'

'How on earth did you know how to do that?' asked Lady Goodroom, a look of disbelief on her face.

'Ach, it's nae bother your Ladymamship. It's easy, I've seen it done on the telly and films tons of times, always wanted to try it.'

'You saw it on the . . .' Lady Goodroom was lost for words. She looked over to Moss who was leaning on his battle-axe.

Moss shrugged and stroked his beard.

'Well I . . .' Lady Goodroom's mouth opened and closed several times. 'Right,' she said, shaking her head, 'well done, anyway. Now see if you can bring Alf out of it.' She turned to John. 'Who sent you here to guard this rock?'

'Nobody *sent* me,' said John. 'I don't know how I got here. I want to go home. I'm starving!' He put his hand into a pocket and pulled out a glass beer bottle. 'An' all I've got is this bottle of very fizzy ale, don't know where I got it – but it's rotten! I can hardly drink it. It stinks!' He looked around. 'Anyone want a drink?'

'Aye,' said Alf, holding out his hand. 'I'll take it, it's no that bad. I finished mine.'

Roger looked at Maddie. She had a hand covering her mouth and was making a *yeeeuch* sound.

'I don't think you should drink—' Roger stopped as the rock-face began to glow blue again.

Moss pushed past John and Lady Goodroom and began running his hands over the rock. 'Look for a small opening,' he said, as Roger and Maddie rushed to help him. 'It is where the dodecahedron key fits the keyhole. Bring light-beams.'

Maddie grabbed the torch from Wullie, just as he snapped his fingers at Alf. The lollipop man looked around with a puzzled expression on his face, and then took a large gulp out of the bottle he was holding. He burped loudly and smacked his lips.

Maddie made another pretend retching sound, and giggled.

Lady Goodroom held John by the shoulders. 'What's the last thing you remember? Tell me and we'll take you home, I promise.'

'Erm, well, I was just going to meet Alf for a beer in the village, like I always do.' He shook his head. 'That's the last thing I remember. Honestly! What's going on?'

'That's right,' sniffed Alf, as Wullie brought him over to join his friend. 'I was going to meet John . . . and now I'm here – *aaatishooo!* What happened to me?'

'I've found it, I think!' shouted Maddie. 'Under this tuft of grass – there's a small opening!'

Everyone crowded round as Moss ripped the clump of grass from the rock-face, and Roger and Maddie shone their torches into the small, smooth hole there. It was at about shoulder height.

'But this isn't the actual portal?' asked Roger, trying to see further in.

'No,' said Lady Goodroom. 'This is the keyhole. The portal only appears at the appointed time.'

'It seems to curve down a little,' said Maddie, pushing Roger out of the way and bobbing her head from side to side, trying to see into the keyhole. 'But I think I can see something in there. If I could get my arm in maybe I could pull out the dodecahedron. Would that work?'

'Do not be a feather-head,' said Moss. 'With the dodecahedron in place, nothing can shift it but the correct spells.'

'Could you do a spell on it, Lady Goodroom?' asked Roger.

Lady Goodroom shook her head. 'No, this is way beyond anything I have in my limited knowledge.'

'I'm going to try,' said Maddie. And before anyone could stop her she slid her hand into the hole.

'*Maddie!*' screamed Lady Goodroom. 'Stop it!'

'It's all right, Aunty,' said Maddie, her arm in the hole up to her elbow. 'It's OK. Just a little bit more and I— *Aaaaaaooooooh!*'

She yanked her arm out of the hole and hopped around, rubbing her arm and moaning.

Lady Goodroom grabbed Maddie's arm. 'What have you done? Show me! Show me!'

Maddie stopped jumping about and let her aunt examine her arm.

'There's nothing there,' said Lady Goodroom, turning Maddie's hand over and back. 'What happened?'

'I felt like I was burnt!' said Maddie, inspecting her hand. 'It's fine now – but I thought it was on fire!'

'You are a stupid fizzgig!' said Moss. 'I told you not to do it.'

'Well at least I tried!' shouted Maddie. 'It might have worked.'

'Step back,' said Moss, and, before anyone could move, he swung his battle-axe over his head and brought it smashing down; the axe bounced off the rock in a huge shower of sparks, but it only left two tiny cuts above and below the opening.

'A bit more warning!' Maddie waved the torch beam in Moss's eyes. 'Crazy dwarf.'

'You were in no danger, Mad-one,' said Moss. 'Nor was the dodecahedron. An army of hardshrewers could not cut through that. We are undone, unless we capture Redcap and get him to reverse the spells.'

'Well, we know where he was,' said Lady Goodroom. She pointed to Alf and John standing huddled together watching what was going on. 'Your last memory was definitely in the village?'

'Aye,' said John, 'walking along the road. We always go to the Greedy Goblin pub, but I don't think I got there.' He shrugged his shoulders. 'Maybe we were abducted by aliens?'

'I think you were,' said Lady Goodroom, nodding. 'But I wouldn't tell anyone about it, if I were you. They might not believe you, it could cause you a lot of trouble.'

'I've probably given them my cold.' Alf chuckled. 'They're probably all deid by now. *Aaatiiishooo!*' He sniffed loudly and wiped his hand across his nose. 'Hope so, the dirty wee— *aaatiiishooo!*'

Lady Goodroom turned to Moss and lowered her voice. 'We get these two back home, I'll do a little mind-spell in the van to help them forget, a quick stop at the cottage, and then into Gifford.' She looked at Wullie. 'William, you phone your friend,' she nodded and winked, 'see if you can get *the supplies*. I'll contact Pen; he'll be waiting on my call.' Lady Goodroom turned to Roger. 'Did you bring a Halloween costume with you?'

'Yes,' said Roger. 'It's in my backpack in the van.'

'Good,' said Lady Goodroom. 'Then you're going trick-or-treating with Maddie and the Captain, after we've made a brief stop at the cottage. William and I will leave there just ahead of you to follow the trail to the Greedy Goblin pub. When we've both finished what we have to do, we'll meet you outside. And now that we've found the portal, plan B is in operation.' She looked at Moss. 'It would be better if you leave your huge battle-axe at the cottage when we get there, Captain, you're scary enough as it is.'

'What's plan B?' Roger tugged on Wullie's sleeve as they all began walking back to the van.

'Eh, well, when I came out the army,' Wullie leaned in closer, 'I worked for a demolition company for a while. If I phone them they might do me a wee favour. We'll just have to see.'

'What kind of favour?' hissed Roger.

'High explosives.' Wullie tapped a finger on his lips. 'Blow that – do-dec-yer-heid-in right out of this world!'

CHAPTER
Nine

'What's the matter, Roger?' asked Maddie, looking back and giggling. She was holding Moss's arm as they walked.

After a quick stop at the cottage for a comfort break, some sandwiches and a drink, they had left the van and were walking towards Gifford village. Lady Goodroom and Wullie were a few minutes ahead of them going towards the Greedy Goblin pub.

'Costume too tight?' Maddie continued. 'Is your skeleton putting on weight?'

Roger raised his face mask and rested it on his head. He pulled at the back of his skeleton costume and wriggled his shoulders before answering. 'I think I've grown a bit since last year.' He caught up with Moss and Maddie again. 'Anyway, at least I'm wearing a costume; you'd hardly know you're meant to be a pirate. All you've got is a scarf round your head and a stick in your belt. And you're wearing an anorak.'

'Don't forget my scar!' Maddie laughed and pointed at the black felt-tip line on her face, crisscrossed with smaller lines. 'Don't forget my scar-har-har!'

'Yeah, right,' said Roger, looking again at the badly drawn scar. He thought it looked more like a large caterpillar crawling up her face.

'Do you have Halloween, Moss, living in your underground places?' asked Maddie.

'Of course,' said Moss. 'We enjoy a celebration of All Hallows' Eve.'

'How do you celebrate?' asked Maddie.

'It is a time of great jollity for us,' said Moss. 'We summon the spirits of our dead ancestors to return to their families. And then we play amusing games to keep them entertained. As if they are watching us.'

'That sounds like a *lot* of fun,' said Roger, making a face at Maddie.

'It is *indeed* fun,' said Moss. 'There is an abundance of fun to be had.'

'Go on,' said Maddie, giggling a little, 'tell us what games you play to entertain your dead ancestors.'

'Many, many games,' said Moss. He thought for a moment. 'I like spin-and-pin, but my favourite of all games is dipping-for-chestnuts.'

They walked along in silence for a few moments.

'OK,' said Maddie, eventually. 'We give in. Tell us how you play spin-and-pin and dipping-for-chestnuts.'

'Spin-and-pin is great fun within a crowded room,' said Moss. 'The more dwarves you have, the greater is the fun. You spin a small dagger or bodkin and whomsoever it points at, then you must jab it in their buttocks.'

Roger and Maddie stopped walking. '*What!*'

'That's mad!' said Roger.

'It is, indeed,' said Moss, chuckling. 'Much madness, much jollity.'

'Is the one who jabs . . . blindfolded?' asked Maddie.

Moss snorted. 'What a stupid question. How would you locate the buttocks if you could not see them?'

'But . . . is it not very sore?' asked Roger. 'And what do the other dwarves do to prevent getting jabbed in the bottom?'

'It is very painful if your buttocks are pierced,' said Moss. 'And you must do everything to stop the jabber. I find that the best way is with a heavy fist-crunch delivered to the jabber's skull area.'

'Wow!' said Roger. 'Some game. And who wins?'

'Oh, no one has ever finished a game.' Moss laughed. 'We just count the dwarves taken to the infirmary to see how much we enjoyed it.'

'And . . . the other . . . the other one, dipping-for-chestnuts?' asked Maddie, quite breathlessly.

'The best of fun,' said Moss. 'Everyone plays. A handful of chestnuts placed in a large basin, and you must retrieve them by using only your mouth and not your hands.'

'Aaah . . . we do that,' said Maddie. 'We use apples though, not chestnuts. That's great fun. And you can get really soaked.'

'How would you get . . . soaked?' asked Moss. 'You must be doing something strange.'

'In the water,' said Roger. 'When you try to get at the apples – or chestnuts – floating in the water, you always get wet.'

'What are you talking about, boy?' Moss sounded puzzled. 'Why would you use water? The chestnuts are lying on the bottom of the basin with fresh, juicy worms on top of them.'

'*Worms!*'

Moss studied Roger and Maddie. He was frowning. 'What else would you use?'

'But . . . but,' began Roger, 'if you put your face in a basin full of worms and open your mouth to get a chestnut . . . then you would . . . swallow . . . a lot of worms.'

Moss laughed and patted his stomach. 'Of course! And sometimes you are so full up with them wriggling inside of you, that you cannot consume anything else for the rest of that day.'

Maddie made a gagging noise. 'OK,' she said, 'that's it, no more questions about disgusting games. What do you do *after* the games?'

'Then we dance and recite poetry until the birds break wind; we eat nuts, syrup-coated scones, and soul-cakes.' Moss paused. 'And we consume tankards of merry-go-down and robberwits wine. We really enjoy All Hallows' Eve, it is a good time for families.'

'I think I'd rather be here,' said Maddie. 'How about you, Rog?'

Roger didn't reply. He was thinking about his own family, his mum and dad and little sister, Hannah. A part of him was now wishing that he'd stayed at home for Halloween. It was bad enough that he had kept his last adventure a secret from them. But here he was again, with more secrets he couldn't talk about.

He was still thinking about his family when he saw lights ahead. 'We're almost there,' he said, pulling his skeleton mask down over his face.

As they reached the outskirts of the village Moss suddenly stopped. 'By the thundering buttocks of the

Auchtermuchty Ogre,' he roared, pushing Roger and Maddie out of the way. He pulled out his sword. 'This place is full of burning goblin heads! What mischief is afoot here?'

'Put that away!' said Roger. 'It's just pumpkins with candles in them. People sit them in front of their houses.' He took hold of Moss's sword arm. 'Look at them! They're not real goblins! It's just a custom we have.'

Moss slid his sword back into its sheath. 'They gave me a startle,' he said. 'You have strange ways of celebrating All Hallows' Eve.'

'You can talk,' said Maddie. 'Eating worms!'

'And sticking knives in buttocks!' said Roger.

'We do not *stick* them in buttocks,' said Moss. 'You hardly need to break surface skin to score. We *jab* them, not too hard.' He thought for a moment. 'Although, sometimes when the game is flowing and the blood is high, the aim of the jabber can go astray. But it's usually just punctured buttocks and legs . . . some broken noses and jaws . . . and ribs . . . arms and legs. Nothing serious.'

CHAPTER
Ten

Gifford was still busy with people enjoying Halloween as Roger, Maddie and Moss reached the village. The first house they came to was lit up with pumpkin-heads and lanterns sitting on the front steps and in the garden.

'Ready?' asked Roger, looking nervously at the other two. 'Remember, Moss, don't say anything, me and Maddie will do all the talking, OK?'

Moss grunted, but nodded his head. He didn't look very happy.

Roger and Maddie walked up the steps and rang the doorbell. The door flew open and a man, wearing a bowler hat, stood in the doorway. There was a red stick-on nose in the middle of his face, and he was wearing a clown costume complete with very large shoes.

'Ah-ha!' said the man. 'Come in! Come in!' He swung round and shouted behind him. 'Little ones! Come and see who's here.' He raised his voice even louder. 'Bring them through, Irene, I'm at the front door.'

Roger and Maddie walked into the man's house and stood in the hall. The man looked closely at Roger. 'You're a skeleton.' He studied Maddie. 'And you're a girl with a dirty face.'

'I'm a pirate,' said Maddie, rubbing her badly drawn scar.

'A skeleton and a dirty pirate!' he shouted, turning away from the door. 'Hurry up, boys!'

There was a scampering noise further down the hall.

Moss shouldered past Roger and stood behind the man, sniffing. Just then a small, fluffy teddy bear and a slightly bigger unicorn arrived, their little faces beaming out with delight from their furry onesies.

'There they are,' said the man, proudly, 'my little angels.' He bent down. 'Look who has come to see you on Halloween.'

The teddy bear and the unicorn were staring at Moss with looks of absolute terror on their little faces.

'What's wrong cherubs?' said the man, turning round to look at Moss. '*Oh, my galloping godfathers!*' he shrieked.

The teddy bear turned round and ran, crying, straight into a small table. He bounced off, sending a lamp and two framed photographs smashing to the floor.

The unicorn sat down where he was and began bawling.

'*What's happened?*'

A woman came running down the hall and picked up the now hysterical teddy bear. Then she saw Moss.

'*Holy—*'

The woman hoisted up the unicorn with one hand and held both howling children tight against her chest. She turned to her husband. 'Get him out of here, at once, or I'll call the police!'

The man's mouth just gaped open and shut.

'Just going!' said Roger, grabbing Moss by the arm. '*Don't say anything,*' he hissed, and then looked at the woman. 'Sorry, he's . . . he's—'

'From Australia!' said Maddie, grabbing Moss by the other arm. 'Our little cousin, from Australia.' She laughed. 'They do things differently there, much more into the whole Halloweeny thing. Take it very seriously. Very realistic costumes. *Bye*! And thank you.'

Roger and Maddie pulled Moss outside. The door slammed shut behind them. They could still hear the crying children as they walked down the path and along the road to the next house.

'Well that went well,' said Maddie, opening the garden gate to let a green ogre and a batgirl come out. She stepped back, holding the gate open for them as they struggled with a large plastic bag that was so heavy it strained its handle.

'Thank you,' said the ogre. 'They give you tons of stuff in that house.'

'Yes,' said the batgirl, as a corner of the bag caught on the gate-catch. 'We've got so much we can hardly carry—'

Moss leaned forward and sniffed at both of them.

The children looked into Moss's face. Batgirl screamed and the ogre jumped back. The plastic bag burst apart, scattering sweets all over the path and pavement.

Roger sighed as he watched the ogre and batgirl run screaming down the road. He looked down at the burst bag and then at Moss. 'It's going to be very difficult, doing this with you.'

'It sure is,' said Maddie, picking up a sweet and popping it into her pocket. 'Come on then, more fun.'

'It'll take us weeks to get round all the houses,' said Roger, trying not to stand on the scattered confectionery. 'We've got to speed this up.'

'If I had not left my battle-axe at the cottage dwelling place,' said Moss, his feet crunching through the sweets as he walked up the path, 'I could smash the doors down and sniff the humans inside. That would not take weeks.'

'No,' said Roger, quickly. 'That's not a good idea, and we're not going back for your battle-axe.'

Moss tapped his helmet. 'I could head-crunch the doors; would take a little longer, but not weeks.'

'*No*,' said Roger, as they reached the next house. 'Just stay back a bit. We'll get them to open their doors, but we won't go in. You stay further back, where they can't see you. And don't speak!'

Moss grunted.

Maddie rang the doorbell. There was a deep *bonging* followed by a wild cackle of maniacal laughter.

'A goblin!' said Moss, unsheathing his sword and pushing between Roger and Maddie, just as the door opened.

'It's just a novelty doorbell,' said Roger, only just managing to keep his footing. 'Put that—'

'*Velcome to my castle!*' said a tall man with two sharp fangs sticking out the sides of his mouth. He was dressed in a long black cloak. 'Who is ring-ging my bell as the witching hour app—'

The man gasped as he caught sight of Moss. His vampire teeth popped out.

Moss shook his sword at the tall man and sniffed loudly. 'There is no goblin here.'

'You nearly pushed me down the steps,' said Roger, squinting angrily at Moss through his mask. 'Watch what you're doing. I told you to stay back.'

The man just stood with his mouth hanging open.

Maddie giggled and held out her hand. 'Trick-or-treat, mister?'

Very slowly, he put his hand into his back pocket and pulled out his wallet. He offered it to Maddie with a shaking hand.

'No, silly vampire,' said Maddie. 'Sweets, not cash!'

The man nodded twitchily. His mouth remained wide open.

'Go get them then,' said Maddie. 'Hurry, hurry.'

He fled down the hall with his cloak flapping behind him.

Roger leaned over and pulled the door shut. 'Quick,' he said, 'run for it.'

'We could make a fortune doing this,' said Maddie, laughing as the three of them ran down the road. 'Moss could get us tons of money robbing people.'

'I do not have the usage for money,' said Moss. 'It is worthless paper and base metal.'

'Give it to me, then,' said Maddie. 'Ah, no, wait; you can do the stones into gold thing, can't you? So that means—'

'Listen!' said Roger, lifting his mask. 'This is definitely not working. All we are doing is causing trouble. And now we've run past lots of houses. What do we do? Do we go back again?' He paused. 'I think we're wasting time.'

'Well, what else can we do?' Maddie shrugged her shoulders. 'We could just chuck it in, and go see how Aunty Gwen and Wullie are getting on? What do—'

'I smell the stench of burning bread,' interrupted Moss, flaring his nostrils as he sniffed. 'It is a goblin for sure.'

CHAPTER
Eleven

Roger and Maddie sniffed the air.

'I don't smell anything,' said Roger.

'Me neither,' said Maddie. 'You sure you're sure?'

'Certain,' said Moss, pointing to a large house on the corner. 'From that dwelling.'

'Now, just hang on,' said Roger, as Moss strode purposefully through the gate. 'Don't go breaking anything. Let's knock on the door first.'

'No time to knock.' Moss bowed his head, preparing to charge at the door.

'No!' yelled Roger, running up the path and round Moss. He stood in front of the dwarf and put both hands on him. 'Maddie, ring the bell! Quickly, before this nutcase does something really serious.'

Maddie ran past and rang the doorbell. Moss shoved Roger out of the way and went up to stand beside her as an elderly, white-haired man opened the door. There was loud music playing in the house.

'Phew,' said the man, waving a hand in front of his nose. 'Can you smell it as well?' He pushed a pair of rimless glasses up on his nose and peered at Moss. 'That's a fine costume you're wearing, sonny, but I'm afraid you can't come in. We're just stopping in a few minutes. It's long past the little ones' bedtime.' He began to close the door.

Moss pushed the door open and barrelled past the old man, sniffing as he went.

'I say, you cheeky young—' the old man tried to grab Moss's arm.

Moss shook him off, and continued walking.

'Sorry,' said Roger, squeezing past the old man. 'He's desperate for the toilet. Can't wait.'

'Hi!' said Maddie, passing the old man. 'I love Halloween, don't you?'

A door opened and a little grey-haired lady appeared carrying an oven grill full of curled-up black things. A great cloud of smoke followed her.

'Hello there,' she said. 'I've burned the scones, I'm afraid.' She peered through the smoke at Moss. 'Which one are you?' she asked. 'Haven't got my glasses. You're Benjamin, aren't you?'

Moss turned to face the door where the music was coming from. He threw open the door and stormed into the room with Roger and Maddie following him.

The room was dark and packed with children and a few adults. Everyone was in fancy dress. And they were all dancing madly and singing 'D-I-S-C-O!' at the tops of their voices; strobe lighting flickered on the walls and ceiling.

Roger and Maddie grabbed Moss by the arms and pulled him back out of the room. They turned to face the old couple.

'I didn't know you were coming, Benjamin,' said the woman, still holding the tray of burned scones. 'Thought your mother said you had a heavy cold.' She coughed. 'I need to get some fresh air, too much smoke.'

'He's an impertinent rascal,' said the old man, 'that's what he is, pushing past me like that.' He looked at his wife. 'Are you sure that's Benjamin, Bella Barton's boy?'

'Of course it is, don't be so silly, I've known him all his life. Your eyesight's getting worse.'

'Thank you very much,' said Roger, hurriedly opening the front door, 'we had a lovely time. Goodbye.' He and Maddie dragged Moss out with them.

'I'm going to have a word with that boy's mother in the morning,' the old man was saying as the door closed. 'Are you sure young Benjamin has a beard?'

'No more,' said Roger, as they made their way down the path. He pulled off the skeleton mask and shook it.

'I'm not wearing this any more and that's the last house I'm doing.'

'Me neither,' said Maddie. 'We'd be better joining the others. Wonder how they're getting on.'

They stood outside the house for a few moments watching as Halloween revellers, children and adults, milled about in their various disguises. There were a lot of superheroes this year as well as the usual sprinkling of vampires, witches and assorted monsters. A group of burly-looking girls in flimsy dresses were standing further up the road at the corner. They were singing rugby songs in very deep voices.

'Your customs are strange,' said Moss, looking at the singers.

'Not half as strange as yours,' said Maddie. 'In case you're wondering, those are men in fancy-dress costumes.'

'I was just thinking that they were not as ugly as the normal female humans,' said Moss.

'Come on,' said Roger quickly, before Maddie could reply to that. 'We'd better get going, we can sniff people as we walk.' He stopped again. 'You know it's funny but I can still smell the burnt scones; it's stronger than ever now.'

'I can smell it as well,' said Maddie. 'And I think it's

83

coming from them.' She pointed at two small monsters crossing the road towards them. They were both in dirty, ripped clothing and wearing hideous rubber masks.

'Halt!' shouted Maddie, standing in front of the monsters as they reached the pavement.

The small monsters stopped.

Roger and Maddie began sniffing them, leaning in close and bobbing their heads round the masks and torn clothing.

The smaller of the two monsters rummaged in his bulging plastic bag and pulled out a large bar of chocolate. 'If you don't stop sniffing me,' he said, his eyes behind the mask fixed on Maddie, 'I'll stick this bar right up your sniffy-snorty nose!'

'Yeah,' said the other monster, looking at Roger. 'And I'll punch *your* nose, that'll stop you sniffing! Now get out of the way, weirdos!'

Roger and Maddie stepped back.

'Sorry,' said Maddie laughing, as the small monsters sauntered past them. 'We're looking for two toddlers with soiled nappies. Thought you might be them!'

'Don't,' said Roger, trying not to laugh. 'They've got a point. We can't go on doing this.' He waved his finger. 'Everyone out here tonight is dressed up in scary costumes. How can we possibly spot a goblin?'

'But the stenching is still there,' said Moss, 'and it *is* stronger.' He took a long sniff, and then pointed to where the singers were standing. 'It is not from the house or the small disguised humans. It is in that direction!'

He started running.

'Hang on!' yelled Roger, following. 'Don't go off again! Wait!'

'No stopping him now!' shouted Maddie, laughing as she ran past Roger.

'Gardyloo, human scrogglings or I'll knock you over!' Moss's voice bellowed out as he pounded along the pavement, scattering startled children.

'Wait for us!' said Roger, and then he gasped and slowed down as he saw what was about to happen.

The rugby players had stopped singing and were watching Moss thundering towards them. One of them, in a pink tutu, placed his beer can on the ground and then crouched down with outstretched hands; the others joined him in blocking the pavement.

'Watch where you're going, liddle fella,' shouted the man in the tutu dress. 'Where's your mummy?'

There was a chorus of shouts followed by great laughter.

'He might go round them?' said Maddie.

But Moss sped up, ploughing straight through the

rugby players like a cannonball through plastic skittles. And went on running.

Roger quickly slipped on his skeleton mask and skipped between the groaning bodies strewn all over the pavement and road. 'Sorry,' he said, trying to make his voice sound deeper so they wouldn't recognise him again. He jumped over the bare legs sticking out of the tutu. 'Very sorry about that.'

'Has he got a team?' the tutu shouted after him. 'Who does he play for?'

Roger didn't answer as shocked revellers rushed to help the injured rugby players.

Ahead, Moss had stopped running. He was outside the Greedy Goblin pub.

Maddie was talking anxiously to Moss as Roger arrived. 'You should wait until we're sure,' she was saying.

Moss was standing perfectly still, staring at the pub and growling. Roger could almost see steam coming out of his ears. The smell of burnt toast was very strong.

Before Maddie could say another word, Moss lowered his head and charged at the doors, slamming them open. He walked straight into the pub. Roger and Maddie had no choice but to creep in behind him.

The noisy pub fell silent. Roger looked round the packed bar. People were standing or sitting as if frozen in time. In the middle of the floor was a huge tin bath, filled with sloshing water and bobbing apples. Beside the bath was a soaking wet man, with a dripping beard. He was kneeling down with his hands behind his back. The floor was covered in wet towels.

In the far corner of the bar, closest to the fire, Roger could see Lady Goodroom and Wullie standing beside a small man wearing a baseball cap. He was sitting at a table absolutely covered in empty crisp packets. Bundles of carry-bags lay under and around the table. The only movement came from the little man, who was hungrily stuffing pickled onions from a jar into his mouth and gulping down the vinegar.

'No children!' The barkeeper, holding a tray of empty glasses, broke the silence. 'It's against the law. You'll need to leave.'

'Just a minute, Hugh,' said the bearded man on the floor. He got up and grabbed a dry towel from a chair. 'Will you look at that!' He dabbed his face with the towel as he spoke. '*That* is ruddy marvellous.' He threw the towel onto the chair and began to clap his hands as he walked towards Moss. 'Son, that's the best disguise I've ever seen in my life. What a get-up, and what an entrance!'

The bar came alive again as people crowded round

87

Moss. Sitting customers stood up and jostled with others to see what was happening.

'That must have cost a fortune, it's brilliant!'

'So authentic-looking.'

'The beard's the best.'

'Look at the detail, the weapons!'

'I smell the burnt-toast stench of a goblin!' said Moss, turning round in a circle as all the faces peered in at him. His hands were on his weapons. 'Where are you? Show yourself!'

'Did you hear that? He even does the voice!'

'Say something else.'

'It always stinks of burnt toast in here.'

'Right, that's enough, you lot.' The barkeeper banged his tray down on a table and jabbed a finger at Moss. 'Out! Now! I'll lose my licence! If the police come round just now—'

'The police are here already,' shouted a voice.

'Aye,' said another voice. 'Sergeant Cameron's sitting in the corner – but he canny get up.'

'Too many toasties!'

The crowd burst out laughing.

Roger looked at the laughing faces surrounding Moss. 'We've got to get him out of here, Maddie,' he said. 'I think he's going to explode.'

'Aunty Gwen and Wullie are coming over to help,' said Maddie, pointing. 'They'll get him out.' The little man was also on his feet, gathering up his carry-bags.

Lady Goodroom and Wullie pushed their way through the crowd and stood beside Roger and Maddie.

'No luck then, Lady G?' asked Roger.

Lady Goodroom did not answer.

'Can you help us, Aunt Gwen?' asked Maddie. 'We're afraid of what Moss might do.'

Lady Goodroom just stared at Maddie. Her face was grim.

'Don't be mad, Aunt Gwen,' said Maddie. 'We couldn't help it, he—'

'Oh, no please . . .' said Roger, as just then Moss began to stride towards the little man with the carry-bags. He had almost drawn his small axe when Lady Goodroom suddenly stepped up and kicked Moss hard on the bottom.

Moss shot forward and belly-flopped into the apple-bobbing bath. A great shower of water flew out, soaking the nearest bystanders. Moss struggled, face down, spluttering and bellowing like an angry walrus.

Then Wullie calmly picked up an almost full pint of beer and poured it over the head of the man standing next to him.

The bar erupted: there was screaming, shouting, laughter; chairs and tables were knocked over, and drinks spilled. The man Wullie had poured the beer over swung a punch. Wullie ducked. The punch struck the bearded man on the nose.

Roger looked at Maddie – she was holding both hands over her mouth – he couldn't tell if she was shocked or laughing. 'Get Moss out of here,' Roger shouted, as the noise around them grew to a crescendo. Maddie nodded, holding back laughter.

Moss was struggling to stand up in the bath. He wrung out his dripping beard and then shook himself like a wet dog. '*Who did that?*' he roared, waving his axe.

'He's got an axe!' someone shouted.

'He's real!' said the bearded man, holding his nose.

'Look,' said another voice, 'he's pulling out a club!'

'Everybody out!' yelled the barkeeper. 'Time please!'

Everyone rushed to the doors. The bar emptied – except for the small man carrying the bulging carry-bags.

Moss stepped out of the bath and stood soaking wet, glaring at Roger. 'Did your wink-a-peeps see the white-livered rutterkin who did this to me?' His voice was low.

'Not-not exactly,' said Roger, desperately looking at Lady Goodroom who was now staring blankly at the wall. He was utterly confused by her actions. *What was she doing?*

Moss's head snapped towards Maddie. 'Did *you* see the perpetrator of this foul deed?'

'Nope!' Maddie's head shook a little; her lips were pursed tight-shut.

Moss stared closely at her. 'Are you snirkling?' He shook his axe.

'Nope!' said Maddie, biting her bottom lip to keep from laughing out loud.

Moss turned to Lady Goodroom, but before he could speak to her, there was a groan from the corner of the bar. Wullie's head appeared from under a pile of chairs and tables.

'What the—' Wullie tried to sit up. 'How the . . . how did I get here? What happened? I was just talking tae that wee man who—'

Wullie's eyes grew wider; he raised a shaking hand and pointed.

'Wh-wh-where did that awfy-looking goblin come from?'

CHAPTER
Twelve

Roger couldn't believe what he was seeing. The small man had vanished, and in his place stood a hideous goblin holding lots of bulging carry-bags in each hand. The creature was about the same height as Moss, with green skin, narrow yellow eyes, and large floppy ears. Its nose was long and pointed and beneath it was a wide grinning mouth full of sharp teeth. Its arms and upper body were unnaturally stretched and its lower limbs were short and crooked. The only clothing it was wearing was a filthy, hooded sweatshirt and badly ripped half-length trousers. A small skull dangled from a chain around its neck.

'Redcap!' roared Moss, raising his axe.

'Dwarf!' screamed Redcap. 'Filthy dwarf!'

Moss kicked a chair out of his way and strode towards the goblin.

Redcap immediately threw his carry-bags at Moss.

Most of them hit Moss on the chest, shattering glass and spilling liquid; pickled eggs and onions bounced on the floor as packets of crisps, nuts and pork scratchings flew everywhere. Moss staggered back, tripping over chairs and knocking into tables. He slammed into a wall beside the door, and his cudgel flew out of his hand. He slid to the floor. Redcap, at amazing speed, bounded over, jumped on top of Moss and pulled out the dwarf's own sword.

'Die, filthy dwarf,' screamed Redcap, raising the sword in both hands.

Moss punched Redcap in the stomach, and then swung his axe at the goblin's head.

'Oooooofffttt!' said Redcap, falling forward. The axe narrowly missed Redcap's head and sliced through the tip of his ear. The goblin gave an unearthly shriek, jumped off Moss and ran out the door.

Moss got up, shook himself, and immediately took off after the goblin.

Roger and Maddie looked at each other for a moment, their eyes wide and mouths open.

'Let's go,' said Roger, snapping out of it.

Maddie closed her mouth.

Outside was pandemonium. People were scattering in all directions. Moss was charging up the middle of the road waving his axe above his head. Ahead of him Redcap was scampering into the darkness.

Roger ran, with Maddie a few steps behind him.

'Wait, Moss,' yelled Maddie. 'Wait for us.'

'Save your breath,' said Roger, slowing a little to let Maddie catch up. 'He's not stopping for anything.'

'Do you think he's heading to the portal?'

'Yeah, sure of it.' Roger glanced at his watch. 'Only thirty . . . thirty-five minutes to go.'

'What'll we do—?'

'I don't know!' shouted Roger, just as he felt the skeleton face mask fly off his head. '*Run!*'

Maddie stuck her tongue out at Roger, and kept running.

They left the streetlights of the village behind them and ran side by side, with only the moon showing them the way ahead. As the road began to get steeper they ran past the cottage with the battered van sitting outside. What had seemed like a very gentle incline when they had walked down it just a short time ago was now a struggle going up.

'The – path – must be around here,' panted Maddie. 'I'm – I'm . . .'

'Me too,' gasped Roger, slowing down and stopping. 'It's here – somewhere . . . all looks same at night.'

'Can you smell that?' asked Maddie, panting and sniffing.

'Yep,' said Roger. 'Toast – strong.'

'There!' Maddie grabbed Roger's arm and pulled him with her. 'Just there, and there's something on the grass too. Look!'

Roger could see a path that led from the main road. And something was sizzling on the damp grass next to it.

'Knew I was right,' said Maddie. She bent low and peered at the ground. 'You can just see the tyre marks from our van. And that's got to be the goblin's blood.'

'It stinks,' said Roger. He looked at Maddie, they were both still puffing. 'You ready to go again?'

'Yeah,' said Maddie. 'You bring a torch, it looks dark?'

Roger shook his head. 'No.'

'Your mobile?'

'Not allowed them at school. You bring yours?'

'Left it on the dressing-table at the cottage.'

'That's bad,' said Roger.

'Yep. But we're still going on, aren't we?'

Roger nodded. 'Oh, yes. We can't go back now.'

Maddie laughed. 'No fun when it's *too* easy. Come on then.'

Roger went into the forest first. The light from the

moon didn't penetrate to ground level and if it hadn't been for the tall trees on either side acting as a guide, it would have been difficult staying on the path.

'Have you any idea where we turned off when we heard Alf sneezing?' asked Maddie after they had been walking for a few minutes.

'Not a clue.' Roger stopped, and turned to the dark outline of Maddie behind him. 'Was sort of hoping you would remember.'

'No idea,' said Maddie. 'Do you want to try here?'

'I suppose,' said Roger. 'The only thing is, it's *very* dark in there. We could get totally lost.'

'We've got to try.'

'OK, let's do it. Hang onto the back of my costume so we don't get separated.'

It only took a few minutes before Roger realised they had made a terrible mistake; he had no idea where they were heading. He was desperately trying to remember where the moon had been when they'd started, but he couldn't even see it now. Branches were hitting them as they stumbled over unseen things on the ground; their progress was painfully slow.

'It's no use,' said Roger, crouching with both hands stretched out in front of him. 'I'm lost. Can't see a thing. This is hopeless.'

'Can you get us back to the path?' asked Maddie, tugging at Roger's costume as she spoke.

'I'll try,' said Roger, turning awkwardly. 'But I'm not even sure if this is the right way.'

They shuffled round.

'Oh!' Roger stopped moving. 'What's that?'

'What?'

Roger could see a blue light in the distance. It was spilling out, filling the forest, spreading towards them.

'*That*,' said Roger.

'I see it,' said Maddie. 'I see it!'

Roger and Maddie stood transfixed as the light kept on coming. It swept over them and continued through the trees until the entire forest was filled in a bright, glowing light; every tree and branch was bathed in blue.

'It came from over there.' Roger pointed this time, and then started to run. 'Come on.'

'Right with you!' Maddie took off after Roger.

They raced through the forest towards the source of the light, dodging round trees, ducking branches and jumping over things scattered over the forest floor. They broke through the final tree line and stopped running. They were standing at almost the same spot as earlier, looking at the same small cliff-face. It was the source of the blue light.

Two figures were locked in deadly combat beside the rock-face. Moss, axe in hand, was attacking Redcap who was defending himself with Moss's sword. The goblin was being driven back under the repeated blows. And Moss was singing!

The goblin dropped onto one knee as the dwarf closed in. Each axe swipe from Moss was harder and more vicious than the one before.

There was a faint rumbling sound; the ground beneath Roger's feet trembled.

Then the blue light went out – completely.

There was another noise – a slight rumble followed by a distinct *click*.

Roger desperately strained his eyes. He could just make out a thin beam of white light streaming out of the rock-face. Moss and Redcap had stopped fighting and were now shielding their eyes from the glare.

The white light was beginning to pull back, sucking itself into the rock-face. It blinked out altogether and apart from the moonlight everything was dark again.

There was a grating noise, the ground shook, and a large part of the rock-face, just to the right of the dodecahedron keyhole, changed into a shimmering portal of twisting colours.

'Wow, look at that!' said Maddie. 'It's beautiful.'

Roger glanced at his watch. 'It's open. It's just after midnight.'

With a roar, Moss charged at Redcap. But now Redcap was frantically trying to battle his way to the portal.

'Come on,' said Maddie, 'let's get stuck into that goblin. I'll karate chop him before he escapes.' She began running down the hill.

Roger groaned and scurried after her.

Maddie circled round the dwarf so she could come up behind Redcap. She slowed, then ran at full tilt and swung her right leg at his back. The goblin, at the last second, turned slightly and stepped out of the way. Maddie missed her target completely and shot past both fighters.

Redcap chuckled as Maddie, unable to stop, flew headfirst through the portal.

Roger could clearly hear a little *'Eeeeek!'* as Maddie disappeared from sight.

The goblin was first to react: he cackled loudly, and then swung the sword at Moss.

Moss just managed to parry the blow. He staggered backwards. Redcap followed him, slashing again and again with his sword.

Roger was scarcely able to believe what had just

happened. He looked at the portal where Maddie had vanished, then back to the fight. He sighed.

'Moss, I'm . . . sorry . . . but . . .'

Roger didn't finish. He ran full pelt at the portal, closed his eyes, and jumped through . . .

. . . and landed on a crocodile.

CHAPTER
Thirteen

At least Roger thought it was a crocodile when he opened his eyes again. It was bright daylight and he was crouching on the back of an enormous . . . *creature*, his hands gripping its scaly back. The crocodile began to lift itself off the ground on *eight* huge legs. Roger wobbled as he tried to keep his balance. *It wasn't a crocodile, it was something much larger.* He looked up just as a massive head on a long neck turned all the way to look back at him.

Roger was looking into the hooded eyes, dripping mouth, and sharp teeth of a monster. He tried to stand up as the beast continued to stare at him. The head of the crocodile-beast moved closer to Roger. Its mouth opened wide, releasing a stinking, putrid smell.

Just then, something smashed into Roger from behind. He went flying off the crocodile-beast and hit the ground hard. He lay, stunned, watching as Redcap quickly got to his feet. The goblin was streaked with blood from his cut ear and holding the now-broken sword.

The crocodile-beast swung its head sideways and began to make for them. Redcap glared down at Roger. 'Die horribly, human!' he screeched, and then he threw the broken sword, turned, and ran. Roger ducked as the sword flew over his head.

The beast kept coming. Roger tried to scramble away. 'No, please!' he shouted. The drooling mouth was just feet away from Roger when yet another figure came flying through the portal. It was Moss! He landed on the crocodile-beast's head, slamming it into the ground. There was a sharp crack as its jaws snapped shut and two of its teeth popped out. Moss hit the ground running, scooped up Roger and, carrying him under one arm, pounded downhill on the dusty, rutted track.

There was a fearful roaring behind them. Roger, head bouncing close to the ground, looked back. The crocodile-beast was chasing, the four legs on each side of its body scooping up great puffs of sand as it ran.

'F-f-f-f-aster, Mo-Mo-Mo-oss,' gasped Roger, now feeling quite sick as he jiggled up and down. It was gaining on them. There was a clanking rattling sound as the crocodile-beast suddenly jerked up into the air on the end of a thick chain round its neck, and flipped over onto its back. It landed hard. Clouds of powdery red sand flew up around its body.

Moss slowed down and turned round. He watched the twitching monster for a moment, and then dropped Roger.

'Ouch!' he cried, as he hit the ground. 'What did you do that for?'

'Where is he?' snarled Moss, looking about. 'Where is that trundle-tail, that whiffling? I'll rip his gizzards out.'

'He's gone,' said Roger, picking himself up. 'You'll never catch him now. He was running really fast.'

Moss stamped his feet, shook his axe, and cursed.

Something caught Roger's eye down the steep slope. His heart lifted. 'Look, I can see Maddie,' he said, pulling at the neck of his skeleton costume. 'It's hot here. *Really* hot.' He glanced up at the sky – and stopped.

There were two suns and two moons. The glare from the suns was intense. Roger quickly looked away. He rubbed his eyes, and began to take in his surroundings. To his right was a village of small, red houses. The houses were very crude affairs; stacked red stone, about two metres high, with flat bamboo roofs and squat doors, and small crooked windows with cloth coverings. All the houses were odd-looking. Bits of them were missing and, while some were reasonably upright, others had completely collapsed. Some of the roofs were broken and long poles, festooned with dirty rags, stuck out through holes. Crude ladders, leading nowhere, jutted haphazardly out of the stone walls, and there were things that looked like upside-down chimneys clinging precariously to the sides of some buildings. The doors in many of the houses were open and goblins were standing in them looking in his direction; several of them seemed to be gnawing at the red stone supporting their own houses. As Roger watched, one of the chimneys dropped off, narrowly missing a munching goblin. Moss bristled beside him.

Beyond the village were fields, and behind the fields were huge red mountains. To his left there was nothing but a wide expanse of desert with more mountains in the distance. And everywhere the landscape was a dusty red, scattered with red rocks and boulders.

'Where are we?' Roger wondered aloud.

'Come and see this, you guys!' Maddie's voice came floating up, quite clearly. 'I came down here to get away from that horrible big monster thing, and found these flowers. They're really cute.'

Maddie was now dancing from side to side, waving her hands in the air. She was in a field of very tall flowers, and she was laughing and letting out an occasional shriek of 'Got me' or 'Missed' as she moved about.

But more of the goblins were coming out of their houses and gathering together.

'This is not good,' Moss said. 'Let us get Mad-one and hasten our departure.'

Roger followed Moss down the track. They reached Maddie just as she was taking off her anorak. 'Too hot!' she said, throwing it on the ground. 'Now watch this.' She danced about some more. The flowers, like large red tulips with ugly gnarled petals, followed her movements. They were swaying and bobbing together, bending over in time with her, or standing up jiggling about as she did. Every few moments one of the gnarled tulips would swell up and spurt out a bubble of clear liquid and then collapse limply on the ground.

'It's water.' Maddie laughed as a bubble hit her on her chest. 'Look!' She wiped her fingers on the liquid and then licked them. 'Try it, it's fun.'

'We've got to get out of here, now!' said Roger, pointing towards the growing crowd of goblins coming towards them. They were all small, undernourished-looking creatures, but most of them were holding large red stones.

'Oh,' said Maddie, seeing them for the first time. 'Didn't notice them there.' She took a step back. 'It'll be OK . . . they . . . seem . . . quiet. I mean look at them, they're all titchy, tiny things, nothing like that big horrible one we were fighting earlier.' Still, she took a few more steps back until she was beside Roger and Moss.

The goblins had gathered together and were silently watching. They were much smaller than Redcap, and light blue in colour. Their mouths and teeth were stained red, and they all had the same nasty, yellow eyes. They were wearing tattered bits of cloth on their bodies, and most of them had dirty rags covering their heads and wrapped around their feet. A few were clutching babies, but they were all eerily quiet.

'See,' said Maddie, out the corner of her mouth, 'they're just shy. I feel sorry for them. You speak to them, Roger. This is your chance, tell them we don't mean them any harm.'

'Why me?' said Roger, trying not to stare at the scrawny creatures in front of him. '*You* do it.'

'You're good at that sort of thing.' Maddie gave Roger a little sideways smile. 'Much better than me.'

Roger cleared his throat.

'Do not be a fopdoodle, boy,' said Moss, in a low voice, swinging the axe in his hand. 'They are *goblins*.'

'No,' said Roger, taking a step forward. He took a deep breath. 'Maddie's right, we've got to try.'

'Do not—' Moss lifted his axe.

Roger raised both hands and spoke loudly. 'Err . . . We come in peace, we mean you no harm.'

The goblins just stood watching. Some of them nibbled on the red stones they carried, their teeth grating and crunching on the rock. Others sniffed the air with disgusted looks on their faces.

'It's working,' hissed Maddie. 'Well done, keep going.'

Roger nodded briefly, and stretched out his right hand. 'We come from a land far, far away, and we are here to help—'

A goblin screeched loudly, and threw a baby at him.

Roger, shocked, just managed to grab the baby goblin in both hands. He held it tightly as it kicked and squealed and wriggled, its sharp, red-stained teeth snapping open and shut as it tried to get at him.

'I warned you of this!' roared Moss, as a stone hit him in the chest.

More stones were thrown; the goblins were making terrible high-pitched screeching noises. Moss and Maddie bent over, trying to shield themselves.

The baby goblin gave up trying to get to Roger's face; it turned its head, and started to gnaw on his sleeve instead. Roger let go of the squealing baby. It fell to the ground and immediately scurried up his leg and started biting at his skeleton costume, shredding his midriff to pieces in seconds. A stray stone hit the baby goblin on the back of its head, and it made a little *ooooh* sound, went cross-eyed, and fell off.

Roger backed away, covering his head as stones rained down.

'The portal!' bellowed Moss, turning. He grabbed hold of Maddie and twisted her in the same direction. 'With all speed!' Several stones thwacked him as he started running, his arms outstretched to shield her.

Roger was struck twice as he began running, but fortunately they were just glancing blows. The awful screeching grew louder.

There was a rattling noise from further up the hill. Moss and Maddie had stopped before the crocodile-beast as it reared up, straining against the chain around its neck.

Roger glanced back. The screeching goblins were still coming up the hill towards them.

'What'll we do, Moss?' screamed Roger. 'We're trapped.'

'We make our stand here!' Moss waved his axe. 'This is the only weapon I have. If *I* fall, use it well.'

The goblins were much closer. The crocodile-beast was jerking on its chain and making gurgling noises.

'Stand behind me for protection,' roared Moss, facing the goblins. 'When they are nearer, I'll attack and slaughter them all, or die attempting.'

Roger and Maddie huddled behind Moss, as more stones were thrown. Moss was singing to himself, thrusting his axe back and forth. 'I go now,' he said, pawing the ground as he prepared to charge.

Suddenly the screaming died away and the stones stopped falling. Roger and Maddie peered over Moss's shoulders. In the distance a large cloud of dust was moving towards them. There was the faint sound of a horn blowing. The goblins scampered back down the hill towards their houses, dropping stones as they ran.

'Come back and face me you whitelivers!' bellowed Moss at the fleeing goblins. 'I'll make you into maw-wallop, you scrogglings!'

'Don't,' said Roger. 'They might come back.' He looked at Moss. 'Are you OK? You got hit by a lot of stones.'

'Fine,' said Moss, pulling a stone out of his beard and flicking it away. 'Bites of a tiddle-fish.'

'Thanks, Moss.' Maddie came round and planted a kiss on the dwarf's cheek. 'You saved me there.'

'Arrrghh!' Moss scrubbed at his cheek with the back of his hand. 'What frippery is this? You do not lip-clap me! I am betrothed.'

'Yes, thanks, Moss!' said Roger. 'Can I give you a *lip-clap*?'

'Only if you have no more use for your head,' said Moss.

Roger thought he caught the slightest smile on Moss's battered face.

The horn sounded again, much closer this time.

'I do not feel that what is approaching will be welcome,' said Moss. 'Come—' He stopped talking as he turned round. The crocodile beast was lying on its stomach watching them closely. It stood up, pawed the ground with its claws, and began swaying its great body from side to side.

'Well we can't go that way,' said Maddie. 'What do we do now?'

Moss looked at his small axe. 'This tiddling is not enough to kill that beast; I need a battle-axe. You should hide until I see what is coming.'

The dust-cloud stopped moving. There was total silence as the dust settled. Then a single horn blasted.

Shadowy figures, wearing horned helmets, began to

emerge from the dust. They were pouring out of three wagons resting on long runners.

'What *are* they?' asked Maddie. 'And *where* do we hide? There's nothing here.'

'They are goblin warriors,' said Moss. '*You two*, make for the fields over there. I'll deal with this.'

'No!' shouted Roger, as more horned figures appeared. 'You can't fight that lot! There's far too many!'

'Go!' yelled Moss. 'They are only goblins. I'll give you time to hide in yonder field.'

Maddie swallowed hard. 'I'll fight with you,' she said, looking nervously at the approaching goblins. 'I can do karate, you know.'

Moss laughed. 'Your katty is of little use against that.'

The goblins had spread themselves out and were advancing towards them, banging their swords against their shields. The sunlight was making their horned helmets and breastplates sparkle brightly.

'Come with us,' shouted Roger. 'Please!'

'Please come,' yelled Maddie. '*Please!*'

'Go now,' roared Moss, and he lifted his axe arm in the air. 'This is how a dwarf fights!' And he charged.

Roger screamed, '*Noooooo!*' as Moss, singing and

shouting war cries, charged down the hill and into the middle of the goblins. The goblins closed around him.

'Come on,' said Maddie, grabbing Roger by the arm. She sniffled. 'There's nothing we can do now.'

Fighting back his own tears, Roger nodded briefly and started running. Behind he could hear the clash of steel on steel and some agonised shrieks.

It was difficult running on the powdery surface, and the heat was relentless. Roger felt as though his lungs were burning as his feet sank into the sand.

They reached the fields and stood gulping in the hot, dry air. The field on their left was full of the large gnarled tulips, while the one on their right was towering bamboo canes.

'Wh-which . . . one?' Maddie could hardly speak.

Roger raised his head. The bamboo offered better cover, but he wasn't sure that they would be able to get through the thick canes.

'Flowers,' panted Roger. He looked at Maddie. Her face was streaked and scarlet from the heat. He tried to smile. 'Ready?'

Maddie just nodded. They ran into the field.

Although they were quite widely spaced, Roger couldn't avoid knocking into some of the gnarled tulips. But he quickly realised that the flowers were also trying to avoid him; they were bending and swaying out of his way as if they could sense his presence.

There was a heavy sensation starting in Roger's lower legs as he ran. He glanced down and saw that there were some blobs of a yellowy gooey substance clinging to his legs. As he watched another blob landed; it seemed to partially sink into the cloth of his costume. The gooey blobs were shooting out from small tubular leaves near the bottom of the gnarled tulips. Most of them floated to the ground and were quickly absorbed, vanishing almost immediately, but a lot of them were now sticking to Roger's legs. Roger slowed down and tried to wipe away the blobs with the side of his hand. He looked at Maddie to say something but could see that she was concentrating hard, trying to place her feet so as not to trample the flowers. Her trouser legs were also covered in blobs of goo.

They were about halfway through the field when a water bubble hit Roger on the face; some of the water ran into his open mouth. It was deliciously cool. He could see the stems of the flowers bulging just before water bubbles burst out of the gnarled tulip heads. More water shot out of the swollen flowers and splashed over him. Maddie had stopped running and was standing in the middle of a water-bubble shower; her arms were outstretched and her mouth wide.

As suddenly as they started, the water bubbles stopped.

Roger sucked on his undamaged sleeve, trying to get a last drop of moisture. Maddie licked at a tiny drop of water caught in her outstretched hand. The crumpled flowers began to stir.

'I think they're filling up again,' said Maddie. 'Look, they're lifting off the ground.'

'Better keep moving,' said Roger, glancing back. There were no more sounds of fighting. He tried to run but found that his legs were now extremely heavy. His costumed legs were covered in the gooey substance. Roger looked at Maddie. She was looking at her own legs and then at him with a puzzled expression on her face.

'It's the flowers,' said Roger. 'They've stuff shooting out of them.'

They slowed to walking pace. Each step became more difficult. Roger felt as if he had lead weights on his legs slowing him down. From the waist down he looked as though he was wearing a mound of small sticky balloons.

'What now?' Maddie looked at Roger. She was struggling to place one foot in front of the other. 'We're nearly there. Look.'

They were almost out of the gnarled tulip field.

Ahead of them was a sandy ridge and just below the ridge was a vast flat plain with towering mountains looming in the distance. Roger stumbled on; he was desperately thirsty. He staggered out of the gnarled tulip field and sat down with Maddie at the edge of the wide plain stretched out before them. The sand was burning hot through his trousers and the gooey blobs, but he needed to rest his legs.

He sat, sucking in the hot air and trying to recover his breath. He looked to his left. All he could see were gnarled tulip fields. To his right were thick fields of bamboo canes, and ahead the valley and the mountains. There was nowhere for them to go.

Roger closed his eyes and lowered his head. He was so tired.

'Look,' said Maddie's voice. 'Look there.'

'What—' Roger jerked upright and opened his eyes. Armed goblins with horned helmets were jogging towards them.

'I can't lift my legs any more with all this gunk clinging to them,' said Maddie. 'Can you?'

'No.' Roger slowly stood up, and held out his hand. 'Not another step,' he said, pulling Maddie to her feet. They stood together, holding hands, as the lead goblin reached them.

It stopped a little distance away and stood sniffing at them as the rest of its party arrived. There was a look of disgust on its face.

'Do you think they're going to kill us?' asked Maddie, in a quiet voice.

CHAPTER
Fourteen

The goblins, close up, were terrifying. They were much bigger than the screechy ones in the village and had dark-blue skin, muscular arms, and wide curved mouths. They were dressed in leathery black tunics and leggings, and they wore short broad boots on their feet. Some of them were quite battered-looking, as if they had been in a fight, and a few were missing their horned helmets.

The leader waited until Roger and Maddie were surrounded, then moved closer, and looked them over. Its teeth were clicking together as the large head twitched from side to side.

'What's happening?' whispered Maddie.

'Don't know,' said Roger. 'Talking to the others, I think.'

'Perhaps it's scared of us,' said Maddie, and she gave a half giggle. 'Its teeth are chattering.'

'So are mine,' said Roger.

The leader stopped clicking and spoke. 'The Mighty

Ruler is commanding you are brought to his exulted pretense. *All hasten!'*

Roger and Maddie looked at each other in amazement.

'What do you—?' Roger stopped talking as the leader pressed the point of his sword close to his face.

'You meant to say exulted *presence*, didn't you?' Maddie shook her head at the goblin. 'Who's a silly goblin?'

'No speaking,' rumbled the goblin. 'Begin to move – now! Torture and health awaiting you at the castle. *All hasten!'*

'Health?' Maddie shrugged. 'You don't torture someone to health. You mean *torture and death.'*

'This is your last warning – no squeaking!' shouted the goblin.

Maddie giggled.

'Do you have any water?' asked Roger.

The goblin's shield shot out and hit Roger in the chest. He flew backwards and thumped to the ground.

'Oh, you dirty big bully!' shouted Maddie.

The goblin raised its sword. 'Have orders not to eat you alive for now, but if you do not do as I smell you, I will kill you and chop your head from your boulders. All hasten!'

Maddie closed her mouth.

The leader went to Roger and kneeled down beside

him. He unhooked a small, leathery pouch from his waist and, before Roger could move, pulled it open and scattered about a dozen little red pellets onto his blob-covered legs.

Two other goblins pushed Maddie down on the sand and did the same to her.

The pellets suddenly grew legs and sprouted teeth.

Roger gasped, but then the pellets began devouring the gooey blobs. They rotated their bodies and moved quickly over the bottom-half of his skeleton costume, even going underneath his legs and appearing again, out of the sand, on the other side.

The pellets moved and ate so quickly that within just a few seconds all the blobs had gone. The little black legs on the pellets vanished, and the leader carefully picked up each one and dropped them back into the pouch.

Roger and Maddie were hauled to their feet and pushed forward.

Roger staggered along holding his arms over his chest – it still hurt where the goblin had hit him, and he was extremely thirsty. Then he thought about Moss, and the pain and the thirst didn't seem so bad. It was incredible to think that he wouldn't see that crazy, maddening dwarf *ever* again. Roger's eyes were filling up and he was blinking rapidly. Maddie bumped into him, winked, and gave him the briefest of smiles.

She whispered, 'Cheer up! We're off to see the Mighty Ruler.'

Roger tried to smile back, but couldn't.

They marched on.

Spindly-legged yellow spiders, the size of small plates, popped out of the sand and stood watching as Roger and Maddie tramped along under the burning suns. Maddie, shuddering, moved closer to Roger; it was her turn to look miserable. 'I *hate* spiders!'

They turned left at the end of the bamboo field, and Roger saw that they were almost back where they had started. The goblin village was on the left and further on he could just see several dark shapes lying on the ground. Roger bit his bottom lip as he realised that one of them was probably Moss.

On the hill above the village, the open portal was shimmering and twinkling on the rock-face. And below, a crowd of goblins was trying to load something on to one of the wagons; they were having great difficulty.

Suddenly a goblin flew out of the wagon and crashed to the ground. There was a mighty roar of '*King Golmar's braces!*' and a figure, with arms tied, leaped from the wagon and rolled down the hill to the bottom. The figure struggled upright as goblins poured down after him. He head-butted the first goblin to reach him, kicked the next two, and scattered the rest with a shoulder charge.

Roger's mouth fell open and Maddie jumped for joy. Half the goblins guarding them started running towards the fight where Moss had just disappeared under a pile of blue bodies.

'All hasten!' The leader clicked loudly, and they began running. Roger and Maddie struggled to keep up. The goblins had no difficulty on the soft ground.

As they reached the wagons, the goblins hauled Moss back up the hill, feet first; he was bound tightly with ropes. Only his head was sticking out, and it was a mass of lumps and cuts.

'*Aaahaa*, the younghedes,' roared Moss's head, as he was lifted and thrown into the back of the wagon. There was a loud crash and the wagon shook. 'I was winning the brangle. I am easily superior to these chitty-faced killcows. If I had my battle-axe I would—' There was a gurgling-spluttering sound, then silence, followed by loud snores.

Roger and Maddie were pushed into the next wagon and sat down on a bamboo bench as goblins piled in beside them. One goblin stood at the front of the wagon. He took hold of a curved horn strapped to his chest and blew on it. Two other horns sounded. The driver then lifted some heavy reins and pulled on them.

121

Roger looked over the side of the wagon, but all he could see were the reins disappearing under the sand. The driver goblin fixed a cloth over his face and then pulled on the reins again. The sand began to stir; long spindly legs broke to the surface far out to the sides of the wagon. In the centre of the legs an enormous yellow body, covered with black spots, rose out of the sand, higher and higher as eight legs pushed it upright. A thick harness was strapped round its abdomen.

'*Ooooo* . . .' Maddie grasped Roger's arm and squeezed. 'It's a . . . spider. The biggest spider in the world!'

'Not our world,' said Roger, his head tilted back, looking up at the colossus towering above him. The creature's legs stretched out an incredible distance on either side of its body. It was lifting and dipping them one at a time, tapping them delicately into the surface of the sand.

Maddie turned her head away. 'This is my worst nightmare,' she whispered. 'I can't look at it.'

The giant spider scuttled forward. The reins tautened and the wagon started sliding over the sand. A great cloud of dust rose as it moved. Roger and Maddie ducked down with their hands over their faces.

CHAPTER
Fifteen

Roger didn't see much of the journey on the bamboo wagon. The dust was thick, and every time he raised his head he could only keep his eyes open for a few seconds. There were glimpses of fields and small buildings, but little else until they began to slow down. Roger peered over the edge of the wagon: he could now see houses on either side. They were built of stone, with narrow, rubbish-strewn lanes between them. All of them were crumbling and dirty, like the crazy houses at the goblin village.

Maddie raised her head and looked at Roger. 'You should see yourself. You're completely covered in red dust.'

'You too,' said Roger, looking at the near-unrecognisable face beside him. The only parts of Maddie's face and head that weren't covered were her eyes.

'Over there,' he said, indicating with a nod. 'I think that's where we're headed.'

'No,' said Maddie. 'I'm not looking at that . . . that *thing*.' She trembled.

'It's OK,' said Roger. 'Just take a quick peek.'

Maddie peered cautiously over the top of the wagon.

Directly in front was a red building with small crooked towers and twisted stonework of walkways leading nowhere, just hanging in the air. There were tattered banners drooping from the walls, all with the same faded outline of a figure on them. And there was a wall round the building, but it made no sense. It seemed to zigzag all over the place, high in some parts and low enough to step over in other places. At one side of the building was a vast open area covered in rows of tents where small figures moved about.

'Think it's meant to be a castle?' asked Maddie, her head down again.

'Dunno, could be,' said Roger. 'Hope Moss is—' He stopped as the first goblin *hissed* at him and shook its shield in a threatening manner.

The goblin driver blew his horn again, and the wagon slowed a little more.

They left the town and continued on the same sandy track, passing more fields. The speed dropped to a walking pace. They pulled up at a long bamboo hut with dozens more of the wagons standing beside it. They all had reins leading under the sand. The spider stood flexing its many leg joints as a crowd of pale-skinned goblins came out of the hut; some were pushing crude wheelbarrows filled with large chunks of steaming flesh and bones. The driver threw the reins to some of the pale-skinned goblins and then jumped from his seat. As the horned goblins started getting off at the rear, the goblins with the wheelbarrows began throwing the flesh and bones onto the sand in front of the giant spider. It was immediately scooped up and devoured with great crunching, squelching noises.

Maddie groaned and looked away.

'Get down.' The leader pointed at Roger and Maddie. 'Your journey with Spot is now over. You must talk to castle.'

'Do you mean *walk* to the castle?' Maddie asked, only for the leader to swing his sword dangerously close to her face.

Roger jumped down from the spider wagon, thinking. *Did that goblin really just call that monstrous spider 'Spot'?*

The horned goblins rolled the unconscious Moss off the wagon and began dragging him, feet-first, towards the castle, where he was hauled over a bamboo drawbridge.

Roger and Maddie, guarded by three goblins with drawn swords, followed him into the castle courtyard.

The courtyard was a hive of activity: formations of well-equipped horned goblins were drilling and marching, other groups were practising their fighting skills or forming shield-walls with impressive precision. An almost overpowering smell of burnt toast hung in the air.

Moss was dragged round the side of the courtyard past the goblin soldiers and taken through a low door and down a long passageway. With pushes from their guards, Roger and Maddie walked behind the snoring dwarf until they reached a large chamber with several archways leading off it. In the middle of the chamber, stacked round a table and chairs, were bamboo baskets stuffed to overflowing with rags. Beside the baskets, on the sand in small heaps, were cudgels, swords and axes, and at the far end of the chamber was a row of empty cells. Three of the cell doors were open and two burly, bare-footed goblins stood beside them. Moss was dumped into the end cell and Maddie and Roger the cells next to him. The iron doors were slammed shut and locked. With a shouted order, their leader led off the horned goblins. Left to their own devices, the guards shuffled over to the table, sat down and proceeded to drink from large tankards and stare at their prisoners.

'Roger!' hissed Maddie. She was sitting in her cell

with her back against the horizontal bars. 'Do you think we could dig our way out of here?'

Roger dropped to the ground and scooped up a handful of sand. 'No, it's too soft. If you take a handful out, it just fills in again.'

'Maybe just as well,' said Maddie, pulling her knees up to her chest and wrapping her arms round her legs. 'I'm too tired to escape. Let's do it later.' She gave a great sigh. 'I'm so glad Moss is alive.'

Loud snores were coming from the end cell.

'Me too,' said Roger. 'They must have drugged him though.'

There was no reply.

Roger looked at Maddie. She was fast asleep. He gazed at her for a few moments, then stretched out his legs and rested his head against the iron bars. He closed his eyes and wondered what his little sister was doing right now. He had no idea of the time in this world, but liked to think that it was bedtime at home and she was listening to a story read by his mum or dad. He was just wondering yet again why he had agreed to a second quest, when he fell into a deep sleep.

CHAPTER
Sixteen

Roger woke up. He was lying on his side with his face in the sand, and he felt awful; his mouth was so dry. It took him a few moments to remember where he was and what had happened. He sat up and looked around the cell as the memories came flooding back. *It was incredible that just a few hours ago he had been . . . Was it a few hours ago, or was it yesterday?* Roger had no idea how long he had been sleeping. He turned his head slightly. The goblin guards were still sitting in their chairs, watching him with their unblinking yellow eyes. Maddie was lying on her side, not moving. He licked at his dry cracked lips with the tip of his tongue and looked at a bucket sitting in the sand, just in front of him.

I don't remember that, thought Roger, as he crawled towards the bucket. *That wasn't there before.* There was a wooden beaker lying beside the bucket.

The bucket was three-quarters full of – *water?* He grabbed the beaker, shook some sand out of it, dipped it into the water, and then raised it to his lips. He drank the entire cupful in three gulps, and then filled it again.

'What you got?'

Roger turned to see Maddie, who was on her hands and knees, peering through the bars at him.

'Water!' said Roger, as he finished off the beaker again. 'There's plenty.'

He lifted the bucket and carried it closer to the cell bars, then filled the beaker and handed it to Maddie. She drank it down, and held out the empty beaker. 'More!'

'See if Moss is awake,' said Roger, handing back a full beaker.

Maddie, still drinking, went over and looked through the bars into the end cell.

'He's still unconscious, but most of his ropes have been removed. It's just his hands that are tied now.' She came back to Roger and held out the beaker again.

Roger and Maddie drank as much water as they could. When they couldn't take any more they dipped their fingers in the water and tried to wash off some of the dust and sand clinging to their faces.

Maddie gave up trying to clean herself and stood. 'I've got a plan,' she hissed. 'You go and stare back at those two creepy monsters. See if you can outstare them.'

'How will that help us escape?' asked Roger, getting to his feet.

'It won't,' said Maddie. 'But it'll help *me*, I need to pee!'

A little while later Roger was dozing when his cell door crashed open. He jerked awake and stared up at the horned goblin standing there. He was very like the leader who had spoken to them earlier. The goblin grabbed Roger by the hair, pulled him to his feet, and then pushed him out of the cell.

'All hasten!' shouted the leader.

Maddie was also being dragged out of her cell.

'Where are we going?' gasped Roger.

'Nowhere,' said the goblin. 'The Mighty Ruler is coming to wee you.'

Horned goblins filled the chamber. They came pouring in through archways and stood to attention around the walls. A goblin, standing beside the table in the centre, raised a horn to his mouth and proceeded to blow twelve long blasts. As the last sound died away all the horned goblins fell to their knees and pressed their foreheads to the sandy floor.

Roger rubbed his head and looked at the kneeling goblins. 'What's going—?' His question was cut short as he was grabbed by one of the burly goblins and forced to his knees. The other goblin pushed Maddie down beside him. Roger tried to struggle but it was no use, he was being held in a very powerful grip.

There was silence. Then . . . a *bang* and a great *whooshing* sound, followed by a cloud of black smoke puffing out of an archway.

There was a great *ooooooo*ing from the kneeling goblins.

Redcap appeared through the smoke. His ear was bandaged now, but he still had that terrible glare.

'No, no, no!' came an angry voice behind Redcap. 'I hadn't given you the order yet! *I* go first! I'm always first. It's *my* grand entrance.'

Roger raised his head, though the goblin holding him tightened its grip. He could now see a second figure had entered the chamber.

It was a man! A tall distinguished-looking man with dark hair flecked with white. He had a sharp nose with a full, curly moustache under it, and his eyes were blue. He was wearing a loose black shirt, and tight black trousers tucked into black boots. There was a curved sword hanging from a broad belt at his waist.

The man waved a finger under Redcap's nose. 'This is not a good start.' His eyes blazed, and he jabbed a finger into his chest. 'Me, first. It's always *me* first.'

Redcap stared back, anger in his eyes. 'I am impatient. I do not wait for what is rightfully mine. I am Redcap, Goblin Chief!'

The man flashed a dazzling smile. '*Of course* you are,' he said, all the temper gone from his face and voice. 'Now let's see what you've brought me.' He looked first at Roger and Maddie on their knees, and then at Moss snoring in his cell.

'Well, well, two humans,' said the man. 'And a dwarf.'

The kneeling goblins were trembling.

'Enough,' said the man. 'I am very pleased. Everybody rise.'

Roger was hauled to his feet. All the goblins were standing rigidly to attention once more. The two goblin guards had their heads bowed. Maddie turned and kicked the one who had been holding her, but it didn't dare move or make a sound.

'So, it's true then! The portal is open once more!'

The man stalked over to Roger and Maddie. He circled them slowly, silently, and then stood before Roger. 'I *do* like what you're wearing,' he said, prodding Roger in the chest. 'A skeleton! How very cheery. I may have something similar made for myself!'

Roger looked down at his filthy, ripped, chewed, skeleton costume, but did not speak.

'This is well done,' the man said, turning to Redcap and nodding his head. 'I should not have doubted you.'

'Then I claim my previous position,' said Redcap, in a rasping voice. 'Goblin Chief.' He pointed to the cell where Moss lay. 'And I want to cut the dwarf into the smallest of pieces and eat him. I hate dwarves, but like the taste of dwarf flesh.'

'Of course you do,' said the man, nodding his head several times, 'of course you do, and you deserve it. All that you want, and more.' He waved a hand casually at the horned goblins gathered in the chamber. 'Now, I know how much you love me, but I must have a few words in private with our guests.' He snapped his fingers. There was a little puff of smoke. 'Out! All of you!'

Every goblin, except Redcap, hurried out of the chamber.

'That's better,' said the man, as the two burly goblin guards ran after the others. 'It's just us.' He pulled up a chair and sat down, staring hard at Roger and Maddie. 'Do you know how *long* it is since I've seen humans? Do you? Because I don't.' He leaned forward and held up both hands. 'I have no idea how long I've *actually* been here.'

Roger and Maddie didn't dare reply.

'*Mmmm,*' said the man, sitting back and hooking an arm over the chair. 'Do you even know who I am? Do you?'

Roger and Maddie shook their heads.

The tall man stood up, held one hand out to the side and gave a deep bow. '*I* am Sir Hugo de Gifford, of Yester Castle.'

Roger and Maddie turned and gawped at each other in amazement.

Sir Hugo sat down again, and waved his hand. 'I had all the prisoners in here killed when I heard that you had arrived. Got it ready for you. Cleaned it up. And I ordered you to be given some of our precious water. Keep you alive . . . at least for now!' He gave a little hiccupping giggle.

'You . . . you're not . . . you can't be *Sir Hugo*,' said Roger. 'It's impossible! He died hundreds of years ago.'

'Hundreds of years ago,' repeated Sir Hugo, standing up and nodding his head slowly. 'It *has* been a long time . . . But I am immortal, I am a god.' He frowned. 'A god stuck in this accursed place, though.' He looked at Redcap and smiled. 'Now, thanks to this wonderful and most useful goblin, one of the few with *any* brains or cunning, I am going to get back to where I truly belong.'

'Weren't you killed?' Maddie asked.

Sir Hugo laughed. 'You cannot kill a god. After the last battle with the dwarves, I escaped my own world before the portal closed and became ruler here.' He held up his hands and looked at them. 'I never get any older or anything!' He nodded. 'It's true. I can do anything. I can burn myself, and I don't feel pain! I can cut myself; I immediately heal. Nothing bothers me – except for the boredom.' He stroked the tips of his moustache. 'But now,' he smiled and patted Redcap on the arm, 'thanks to this *excellent* fellow, I can return to my world and rule there. And he can rule where he belongs.'

'We will have our revenge on the dwarves,' said Redcap. 'We shall kill all of them, and eat them with pickled onions.'

Roger and Maddie exchanged glances as Redcap continued talking.

'I was returning with the lovely salty-pickly things when *they* stopped me.' Something like saliva dribbled out of the corner of Redcap's mouth and dripped onto the sand. It sizzled briefly. 'Soon I return with the new goblin army, kill them all, and feast on their flesh dipped in briny juice and salty peanuts.'

'Yes, yes, of course you will,' said Sir Hugo vaguely, a look of disgust on his face as he watched the drool dripping from the goblin's mouth. 'But *I* need to prepare the army, before I hand over control to you, Redcap.' He laughed. 'It's a never-ending business, I keep training them, and they keep dying off! I turn my back for a moment and they've turned into old goblins. Got to have them killed to make room for new recruits, and then I have to start all over again.' He shook his head and shrugged. 'I don't really mind, I do *like* killing things; it's really my greatest pleasure – apart from torture. Can't feel pain myself, but I love to see others suffer. Watching them is . . .'

He broke off, muttering to himself, clenching and unclenching his fists.

'Right,' said Sir Hugo, coming out of it. He smiled at Roger and Maddie. 'My goodly friend here,' he pointed at Redcap, 'tells me that there have been many advances made since I was last in my world. He tells me of great buildings reaching to the sky, carriages without horses *or* spiders to pull them, and blazing candles that do not need to be lit.' He rubbed his hands together. 'Is all this true, can carriages move by magic alone?'

'Oh, yes,' said Maddie, 'all true. We've got motor cars, and ice cream, and television.'

Roger coughed.

'What is this tel-e-vis-ion?' asked Sir Hugo, his eyes fixed on Maddie.

'I have told you this!' shouted Redcap. 'You are wasting time on questions I have answered. Let us go now! We must slaughter humans and dwarves.'

Sir Hugo's jaw tightened. He appeared to be fighting to control himself. He breathed deeply and looked down at his boots. 'It's so difficult to keep them clean in all this dirt and sand.'

His face relaxed again, and he bent and brushed some specks of sand from his toecap, then straightened up and smiled at Redcap.

'Yes, you did tell me,' Sir Hugo went on. 'You certainly told me.' He looked back to Maddie. 'But it cannot be true, *a seeing portal in every dwelling place*? Humans can look into other worlds?'

'Yup,' said Maddie. 'Anywhere we want; just press a button and we're off, boldly going, seeking out new worlds.'

Roger groaned.

'This I must experience for myself,' said Sir Hugo. 'The magic must be very powerful. Is mo-tor car a mighty weapon?'

'No, no,' said Maddie. 'It's a sort of carriage, but much better. It takes people under the sea so that they can visit mermaids and have parties with seaweed ice cream, and talk with lobster-men.'

Sir Hugo gasped. 'This is wondrous indeed.' He pulled at his moustache for a moment, and then pointed at Roger.

'Have they got a huge, highly-trained army equipped with the sharpest swords and hardened shields?'

'I have also told you this!' thundered Redcap. 'Why do you persist in questioning? Do you not trust *me*, the Goblin Chief? Kill them! Be done with them. *Do as I say!*'

Sir Hugo bent down and slipped a hand into the top of his boot. His mouth was opening and closing without any apparent reason. He straightened up and, holding his arms outstretched, turned to Redcap. 'Do as *you* say! Well, my good and faithful old friend and ally, without you none of this would be happening. And you've been so patient.' He giggled a little and looked into the goblin's yellow eyes, smiling. 'Do as *you* say! Well, it is my pleasure to reward you for all that *you've* done.' He put his arms on Redcap's shoulders, and pulled him close. 'And your reward is' – he whispered in the goblin's uninjured ear – *'a quick death!'*

There was a gurgling from Redcap as he slid from Sir Hugo's grasp and fell to the floor. There was a small dagger sticking in his back.

CHAPTER
Seventeen

'Did you think that you could return here after an eternity and become ruler of my army?' screamed Sir Hugo, his eyes bulging and veins visible in his neck. 'You fool! No one remembers you. No one even knows who you are. *I* barely remember who you are! There is only room for one immortal here.' He took a deep breath and shouted again. 'You enter a chamber first, before *me*! You interrupt *me*! You tell *me* what to do!' He took another gulping breath. 'You want to become Goblin Chief, in charge of *my* army! *I* train the army! *I* rule this world! Everyone obeys *me*! I am the *Mighty Ruler*!'

He stopped ranting and stared at his shirt. 'Ah . . .' he said, flicking at the shirt with his fingers. 'You've got blood on me. Bad goblin! I'll need to go and change this.'

'Why—?' Roger started to speak, but his voice was hoarse.

Sir Hugo spun round and beamed at Roger and

Maddie, all the anger gone from his face. 'Ah – I forgot you were there!' he said in a very calm, friendly voice. Then he pulled the curved sword from his belt. 'I'm going to kill you. Might as well do it now in case I get any more blood on my clothes.' He laughed. 'Can't be changing shirts all day, eh?'

Roger stepped protectively in front of Maddie. He was shaking. 'Why are you *like* this?'

Maddie shoved Roger to one side and glared at Sir Hugo.

There was a low growl from the cells. 'He cannot understand that question,' said Moss's voice. 'He is a fopdoodle, a snirtling killcow, his brain inhabits different worlds.'

Roger and Maddie both turned at the same time. Moss was now standing in his cell. His hands were tied together, and he looked awful.

'Can you not see?' Moss rattled the bars of his cell. 'There is no connection with sanity. His one brain is sitting on two chairs.'

'The dwarf!' shouted Sir Hugo. He shoved his sword back into his belt and clapped his hands. 'I nearly forgot the dwarf.' He crossed to the cell and stood looking at Moss, tapping the fingers of one hand on his mouth. 'Now then, what to do first, *mmmm*?' He stood thinking and

140

tapping for a few more moments, and then spun on his heel and walked back to the chair and sat down. He sniggered, and wagged a hand backwards and forwards. 'Who to kill first, who to kill next, who to torture . . . the decisions are endless.' He looked at Moss. 'I think I shall torture him.' He thought for a moment, and scratched his head. 'Or kill the children first, *then* torture?' He bit at the knuckle on his index finger. 'No, no, no! Torture first! Always torture first.' He bounced to his feet and rubbed his hands. '*Guards!*'

The two guards appeared. They kneeled down with their foreheads touching the sand.

'Up, up,' said Sir Hugo, flapping his hands. 'Things to do.' He pointed at Redcap's body. 'Give me my dagger, and then get rid of *that*, then ready the torture chamber.' He walked back to the cell with Moss, and stood twirling the ends of his moustache. 'Now . . . *mmmm,* what to do with you, something special . . . I have a memory about something dwarves really hate, but can't quite put my finger on it.'

'Do your worst, trundle-tail,' snarled Moss. 'I'll not bend a knee to the likes of you.'

'Bend a knee . . .?' Sir Hugo raised a finger and wagged it at Moss. 'No, *no*! I do not want you to do anything like that. I just want to torture you.' He laughed

141

and leaned a little closer. 'So, is there anything – just between the two of us – that you particularly dislike, *mmmm*? You know, something you *really* fear?'

'I fear nothing!' roared Moss, pressing his face against the bars. 'I am Mossbelly MacFearsome!'

'*Oooh* . . . right.' Sir Hugo nodded, and put a finger on the side of his head. 'You're sure now? I've got an old memory, lodged here.' He tapped his head. 'You can trust me, I won't tell anyone else, promise.' He looked at Moss for a moment. 'No? Oh, well . . . don't worry, it'll come back to me.' He turned to Roger and Maddie. 'I hate it when something's there, but you just can't remember, don't—?'

Sir Hugo stopped talking as he caught sight of himself in one of the tankards sitting on the guards' table. He bent closer and smiled at his reflection – smoothing his eyebrows and checking his teeth. 'Do you like my trousers?' he said, straightening up again. He shook his hips.

Roger and Maddie didn't reply. They could only watch as the preening dandy raised his arms and waggled his hips again.

'Goblin skin.'

Nobody spoke.

'They're all different colours, you know.' Sir Hugo lowered his hands and patted his thighs. 'The goblins I mean. Have you noticed?' He rubbed his thighs. 'They are good, aren't they? I have very good tailors. And I kill one every few months, just to keep them on their toes.' He gave a little spin round.

'*Yeuch!*' said Maddie.

'And some parts of goblins are fairly edible,' continued Sir Hugo. 'I'm particularly fond of their big ears, fried crisply, for supper.' He smacked his lips. 'Delicious! Got to be careful how you cook them though, they burn very easily.'

Roger looked at Moss. The dwarf gave the slightest shake of his head, as if warning Roger not to speak.

'Now then,' said Sir Hugo, 'got to get on. I'll just put you back into your nice comfortable cells. Would love to talk some more, but an awful lot to do. And I'll have to change into something a bit more warlike.'

He shouted and the chamber filled with horned goblins.

'I'm so very proud of them,' said Sir Hugo, as the goblins lined up. 'All hand picked, my elite troops. I even taught them to speak our language. It's taken a long, long time but they're getting there . . . well, some of them. I'm really quite a benign god. And they'd do anything for me in return.'

'Why do they all obey you?' Roger asked as his cell door slammed shut.

'Yes, there's tons of them and only one of you,' said Maddie, from her cell. 'They could easily beat you.'

Sir Hugo put his hands on his hips. 'Because I can perform miracles. Watch this!' He whirled round and clapped his hands.

He walked along the line of the elite horned goblins. 'Who wants to see a magic miracle?'

There was a gasp from the goblins; some started trembling.

Sir Hugo stopped at a goblin. 'You?'

The goblin dropped to its knees. 'Oh, yes, Mighty Ruler. Do the spider out of the helmet; that is a blunder to behold. We all love that one.'

'No, too simple,' said Sir Hugo, frowning. 'Come now; stand up. Choose something better.'

The goblin stood up. There was a look of terror on its face. 'Please, Mighty Ruler, spider out of—'

'No!' snapped Sir Hugo, his face darkening. '*Something* else!'

'F-find the spider under one of the three tankards?' stuttered the goblin.

Sir Hugo narrowed his eyes, and then stuck his hands behind his back. 'Right,' he said, 'you've chosen Pick-a-Hand. Now! *Pick a hand!*'

The goblin, visibly shaking, pointed at Sir Hugo's right side.

Sir Hugo brought out his right fist and stuck it under the goblin's nose. The goblin squeaked and pressed back against the stonework.

'Oh, don't be such a scaredy-spider,' said Sir Hugo, lowering his hand a little. 'It's nowhere near you. You'll be fine.'

He flicked his thumb against his index finger. Nothing happened.

'Wrong hand!' shouted Sir Hugo. 'You lose!'

The goblin gasped and bowed his head in relief as Sir Hugo moved onto the next goblin in the line.

'Your turn,' said Sir Hugo, both hands behind his back again.

The goblin gave a little sly grin and pointed at Sir Hugo's right side.

Sir Hugo took out his hand, stuck it under the goblin's nose, and flicked his thumb again. A small flame appeared on the end of his thumb.

'You win!' shouted Sir Hugo. 'Now you get to blow it out. And if you succeed with one puff, you get promoted. Fail, and it's the mountain quarries for you.'

There was a collective gasp from the goblins. The

one with the flame under his long nose tried to turn away.

'Stand still,' snarled Sir Hugo. 'You're the winner. You get to—'

The flame on Sir Hugo's thumb suddenly roared up and touched the tip of the goblin's nose. Its entire body was immediately consumed in crackling flames; in seconds the goblin blazed white-hot. The horned goblins on either side fell over each other as they fought to get out of the way.

'*Oooops!*' said Sir Hugo, laughing. 'That's not meant to happen . . .'

The flames died as quickly as they started. All that remained of the goblin was a stain of dark ash on the sand. A little cloud of oily smoke drifted off down one of the passages.

'Oh dear,' said Sir Hugo, blowing out his thumb, 'perhaps I should have tried the spider out of the helmet.' He looked at the cowering goblins. 'It's your own fault anyway,' he suddenly stormed. 'Your skin is far too greasy. Now get out, all of you! Go! Now! I'm getting angry. Look!' He pointed down at his boots. 'There's hot grease on them, they're *ruined*.'

As the goblins began to rush out of the chamber, Sir Hugo stepped closer to the prison cells and put a hand to the side of his mouth. 'They really are the most incredibly thick creatures,' he said, smiling again. 'So stupid. Almost no brains; they do anything I tell them.' He sighed. 'But then, as a god, I have to show them how powerful I am, to rule them.'

'By the bearded goats of Kinloch Rannoch!' shouted Moss. 'You are not a god! You are a pustule on my buttock-rump. You use the simplest of trickery to fool these whifflings. And only the very worst fopdoodle would kill his own army!'

Sir Hugo slowly turned to Moss and held up a finger. '*Aaahaa . . . bearded* goats, that's it! Well done, dwarf. I've remembered what all dwarves fear the most.'

He moved to Moss's cell and stood close to the iron bars. 'I know what I'm going to do to you.'

'I fear nothing!' roared Moss. 'Nothing in my world or this pit of evil frightens me. Do you hear my words? Nothing!'

Sir Hugo leaned a little closer. He smiled. 'I . . . am . . . going . . . to . . .' His voice dropped to a whisper.

Roger strained to hear, but couldn't make out what he was saying.

Sir Hugo finished talking and straightened up again.

Moss stood still for a moment. 'No,' he gasped. 'You would not do that.'

Sir Hugo didn't speak. He just nodded and smiled.

Moss stepped backwards. 'No,' he said again. His heel dug into the sand. He fell back, and sat down. 'Not *that*.'

Sir Hugo kept nodding and smiling, and then shouted: 'Take him to the torture chamber. And make sure that the knives are blunt. Very, very blunt.'

CHAPTER
Eighteen

'How long do you think he has been away?' asked Maddie.

'Don't know,' answered Roger, for the umpteenth time. He shook his wrist with the watch on it. 'I told you this is not working properly. It's going, but so slowly, it's hardly moving.'

Roger was sitting looking at Maddie in the cell next to his. It seemed like hours since Moss had been dragged away, struggling and cursing, through one of the archways. The two goblin guards were hunched over the table eating noisily off two thick rock plates that were piled high with wriggling beetles and bugs.

'How do we get out of here?' Maddie stood up and shuffled to the front of the cell and took hold of the bars. She shook them. 'Have you thought of anything yet?'

'No,' said Roger, wearily. 'Have you?'

'When I get out of here I'm going to karate the two of them to pieces,' said Maddie, nodding at the goblins.

She shuddered at the crunching noises coming from the table. 'Look what they are stuffing into their faces.'

'I hope Moss is—'

'*Yeeeuch!*' Maddie let go of the bars as if they had turned red hot. She stepped back. 'Look at that now!'

Roger jumped to his feet and rushed over. Both goblins were squatting with their breeches around their ankles. They were each placing a bottle under their bottoms. There were loud *braaapping* noises, before the now fizzing bottles were placed back on top of the table.

Suddenly there came the sound of footsteps and Sir Hugo appeared, followed by eight horned goblins. They were carrying Moss face down.

The goblin guards pulled up their breeches, rushed over to the end cell and opened the door. Moss was thrown in. He lay there, not moving.

'Now *that* was fun,' Sir Hugo said. 'I really enjoyed myself.' He giggled. 'Can't say the same for the little dwarfy. Must go now, lots to do.'

Roger was almost in tears. 'Is Moss . . . dead?'

'What?' Sir Hugo stopped. 'Dead? No, he's still with us, the stubborn little . . . I'm just getting started with him.' He frowned at Roger. 'Hmmm . . . Do I kill you now? Or later? Can you remember?' He tutted. 'Memory, eh! Must be getting old.' Breaking into hysterical laughter, he clung to the cell bars, almost sobbing. 'Oh, how I amuse myself.' He stood and turned. 'I really have an awful lot to do before conquering the Earth. And I'm ravenously hungry! All this torturing.' He waved a hand over his shoulder as he left the chamber. 'Executions to finish . . .'

The goblin guards waited for a few moments, and then dropped their breeches again.

'Moss, Moss!' shouted Maddie, running to the iron bars that separated her cell from the dwarf's. She pressed against them with her arms stretched out, trying to reach him. 'Are you all right? What did he *do* to you?'

There was a low groan from Moss.

'Mossy!' shouted Roger. 'Show us what he did. Turn over.'

Braaap! Braaap! Braaapp! came from the goblin's table.

Moss rolled over.

Roger and Maddie both cried out in horror.

Moss's beard was gone!

CHAPTER
Nineteen

Maddie took several steps backwards and put both hands up to her mouth. Roger held on to his cell bars and stared in disbelief.

'Oh, no!' Maddie gasped. 'What has he . . .?'

Roger couldn't speak. He gripped the iron bars tighter and watched as Moss got up, shuffled over, and stood facing them. His luxuriant beard and moustache had been completely removed. The top of his face was the same: weather-beaten, warty, and covered in faint blue lines. But the rest of his face – streaked with blood – belonged to someone else. His skin was a pasty, puckered grey, with a yellowish tinge, and there were cuts all over it. To Roger it seemed like two different faces had been stuck together. And he couldn't help notice that Moss's top lip was quite prominent.

'This is what he did to me,' said Moss in a quiet voice. And then he turned and went to the back of the cell and sat down.

152

'It's . . . it's not too bad.' Roger managed to croak out. 'Er . . . it makes you look . . . ehm . . . younger.'

'You look *awful!*' said Maddie. '*Ooops!* I mean you look . . . awfully different. Yep, different – well, you know what I mean.'

'I know what you mean, Mad-one,' said Moss. 'Now leave me to my own company. Do not engage me further. I need hudder-mudder time.'

'No, Moss, talk to us,' said Roger, glaring at Maddie, who was making faces and shaking her head. 'It's not that bad.'

There was no reply from Moss.

'Come on, Moss,' said Maddie. 'It's just a beard, don't let it bother you.' She walked to the back of her cell. 'I never liked your beard anyway; horrible dirty, scratchy-looking thing.' She smiled. 'In fact I *hate* beards; they should all be banned. There! Do you feel better now?'

Moss lowered his head onto his knees.

Roger stuck his arm into Maddie's cell and beckoned frantically at her.

'What?' Maddie leaned against the iron bars next to Roger. 'I *do* hate beards. They look stupid, particularly the grey stubbly ones, they're really gross.'

Roger reached through and gently pulled Maddie

down until they were both sitting on the sand together, with only the iron bars between them. '*Shssssh*, Maddie,' he whispered. 'I know you're trying, but you're only making it worse. Let's just leave him alone.'

'I just said—'

'No, really, let's just leave him. What's happened to him is very bad.'

'I was only trying to help.' Maddie pressed her face between the bars. 'He'll never get *it* back, you know,' she said, her voice barely audible. 'Takes them tons and tons of years to grow *it*!'

'That's even worse,' said Roger. 'He'll need time to recover from this. And we can't count on him to help us now. We've got to get out of here by ourselves. You got any ideas?'

Maddie thought for a few moments, then looked at the two guards. They had finished their meal and drinks and were both sitting back in their chairs with their eyes closed and their open mouths flapping noisily as they snored. She raised a finger and pointed at a ring, with one large key on it, lying on the table.

Roger nodded. 'I see it,' he whispered. 'Have you got an idea?'

'Yes,' said Maddie, 'I could try levitation.'

Roger made a face and gave his head a little shake.

154

'Could you really do it? I thought you weren't very good at it?'

'I *am* good at it!' said Maddie crossly. 'Well, *quite* good. Not as good as Aunt Gwen, but still OK. What else are we going to do to get out of here?'

'I've got nothing,' said Roger. 'Go ahead then and try, but you'll need to be very careful.'

'No!' Maddie glared at Roger. 'Really? Never thought of being *careful*.' She shook her head. 'I hate it when people say stupid things like that.'

'Quiet!' begged Roger. 'Don't speak so loudly; you'll wake them. And I was only trying to help.'

'Well don't,' said Maddie, whispering again. She got up and walked to the front of her cell and stood for a moment, before turning to face Roger. 'I'm sorry for losing my temper just now. I *will* try, but what if I mess this up? We'll never get out of here. We could die in here.'

'Butter me no buts,' said Roger, sternly, and in a deep whisper.

Maddie put both hands over her mouth and started giggling. She made tiny squeaking noises as she tried to muffle her laughter. Roger tried not to laugh too.

'Even . . .' Roger said when he'd recovered, 'even if the key falls, it'll land in the sand, so it won't make a noise. You'll do it. I know you will.'

155

Maddie took a deep breath in – held it – and then slowly breathed out.

'You OK?' Roger asked.

Maddie nodded with her mouth tightly shut. She kneeled down, fixed her eyes on the key, held up her hands and flexed her fingers. Roger stood and watched the key.

Maddie turned her hands over with her palms facing upwards and began speaking very softly. '*Flankenpoop-blankenmix-zrrifflegug.*'

Nothing happened.

Maddie shook her hands and looked up at Roger.

Roger smiled back and nodded encouragingly.

Maddie tried again. '*Flankenpoop-blankenmix-zrifflegug.*'

Nothing happened.

Maddie lowered her head and mumbled to herself, the same words over and over. She gasped, and raised her head.

'*FlankenPOP-blankenmix-zrifflegug!*'

The key moved. With a little tinkling sound it swung up in the air, quivering gently just above the table. The goblins continued to snore.

'You've got it!' whispered Roger. 'Well done! You pooped when you should've popped!'

The key dropped back onto the table.

Maddie glared at Roger. 'Don't make me laugh!'

Roger made a face and mouthed a silent *sorry*.

One of the goblins opened his eyes, snorted, and then closed them again. He crossed his legs and wriggled his shoulders into a more comfortable position.

Roger and Maddie remained motionless.

Maddie looked up at Roger.

Roger just shook his head.

The goblin began to breathe deeply.

Maddie looked at Roger again.

Roger gave the tiniest nod.

Maddie started again.

'Flankenpop-blankenmix-zrifflegug.'

The key and ring lifted off the table, and began to move – very slowly – towards Maddie.

Roger stopped breathing as the key floated clear of the table. He was desperate to say something, but was terrified that he would break Maddie's concentration again.

The key dipped suddenly, almost touching the goblin's crossed knee, it came back up again, swung to the right, back left, and then steadied.

Roger, his knuckles white on the cell bars, breathed a sigh of relief.

Then the key dropped out of the air and landed on the goblin's outstretched foot.

Maddie jumped up beside Roger and grabbed hold of the bars. They both watched as the goblin's foot began to bend down towards the sand. The key slithered between the goblin's toes and dropped off. As it fell, the keyring hooked itself round the big toe. The key jerked to a halt, dangling from the goblin's foot.

Maddie turned and looked at Roger. '*What now?*' she said, silently.

Roger shook his head. '*Don't know.*'

The goblin wriggled back in his chair and uncrossed his legs. The keyring flew off his toe and landed in the sand. The goblin began to snore again.

Maddie quickly kneeled down.

'Drag it through the sand, Mad-one,' said the quiet voice of Moss.

Roger and Maddie turned. Moss was in the front corner of his cell next to Maddie. 'Drag it to me, Mad-one.'

Maddie nodded.

'Bring it, but with care, to my place of incarceration,' said Moss, taking a step back.

As Maddie made curling motions with her fingers, the key slowly began to move through the sand. Moss waited until the key was within reach, then he bent down, hooked a finger through the ring, and stood up. He put the key into the lock, and turned it. The door squeaked open.

He stepped out of the cell, and crossed noiselessly to the table. He stood looking at the sleeping goblins for a moment – then swung his fist at the first goblin. There was a dreadful crunch as Moss's fist connected, sending the goblin flying across the chamber. The second goblin's yellow eyes snapped open just as Moss brought one of the bottles from the table crashing down on its head. As the goblin slumped over the table, Moss picked it up and threw it down beside the other one. A terrible smell rose up from the liquid in the broken bottle.

'Now,' said Moss, walking to Roger's cell with the key, 'I have been greatly angered!'

CHAPTER
Twenty

'What are you going to do?' asked Roger, as Moss released Maddie. He was finding it difficult to look at the dwarf; he was so different, not like the *real* Moss.

'I shall kill goblins and the human,' said Moss, selecting a cudgel and an axe from a pile of weapons. 'You and the Mad-one go to the portal. Seek out our friends on the other side and await the arrival of our army.'

'And what happens then?' asked Maddie, picking up a dagger.

'The dwarf army invades, destroys any goblins still alive, returns home with my bones and buries them, with full pomping ceremonial, beside Bloodbone Knottenbelt.'

'So you're going to be dead, then?' Maddie said. She tested the point of the dagger on a finger, and then mouthed, '*Ouch!*'

'Of course,' said Moss. 'I shall destroy many within this castle, but to be straight-fingered with you, the vast army on the outside may prove a tad too much even for me.'

'It's a rotten plan,' said Maddie, sucking her finger. 'We should all escape together.' She stuck the dagger in her belt, and handed a small rusty axe to Roger.

Moss raised a hand to his chin. 'I cannot return home like this, there is no place for me there. Far better to fall in battle than face snirkling and shame.' He dropped his head. 'And my beloved Queen would not wed the ugly stoop-gallant I have become.'

'Well, you're certainly no oil—'

'I agree with Maddie,' said Roger, quickly. 'Your plan has a big flaw in it.'

'What?' Moss looked puzzled. 'I see nothing amiss.'

'Ah,' said Roger, thinking fast. 'But there is something that you have not considered, and that is . . . You haven't thought about what stupid younghedes me and Maddie are!'

'Hey!' Maddie glared at Roger.

'I do not follow this wording of yours,' said Moss.

'Well,' said Roger. 'You're off slaughtering goblins and the two of us,' he pointed at Maddie and himself, 'escape, right?'

Moss nodded.

'How could we, eh?' Roger held up his hands.

'Without you to lead us, we'd have no chance. You are the only one who could get us to the portal. Without you we'd be lost before we got started. We need you to take us there.'

'And once you've got us there,' said Maddie, '*then* you could get yourself killed. You could die fighting that monster guarding the portal. That would be a really good way to go.'

Roger frowned at Maddie, who smiled sweetly and stuck out her tongue.

'You are correct in this,' said Moss, after a few moments. 'I have now given it more thinking time, and you are right, without me you would get lost going from your nose to your mouth. We go to the portal together.'

'Thank you,' said Roger, 'that's great.' He pointed at the baskets of rags. 'And I've got an idea to get us out of here, without having to fight.'

'You're a cunning Destroyer, Rog,' whispered Maddie, as they started pulling rags out of the boxes.

'A female washer goblin?' asked Moss, again. 'I am a goblin who washes clothes?'

'Yes,' sighed Roger. 'I've already told you this, several

times. We are all washerwomen—I mean, washergoblins.' He shook the basket he was carrying. 'This is our disguise, and the rags we are carrying in the baskets – are for washing!'

'Why am I a *female* washergoblin?' asked Moss, stopping again.

'Sorry,' said Roger, *'that'*s a mistake. You're a male washergoblin! Please, just act like a goblin who washes clothes. You're always telling us what a great actor you are.'

Moss grunted. 'You have the truth; I am very good at adopting the manner of another. My skills are indeed great.'

'This really stinks,' said Maddie. 'I think whoever had these clothes before us must've died in them.'

'I'm pretty sure they did,' said Roger, looking at Maddie standing just in front of him. They were halfway along the passage from the chamber, and Maddie was covered in dirty rags from the top of her head to her feet. And she was right; the rags they were wearing did smell awful.

'Something approaches,' said Moss. 'Cover your faces.'

Roger could see a horned goblin hurrying towards them. He was carrying a stack of empty baskets.

The goblin stopped in front of them, *clicked* and gave a little screech. Maddie immediately *clicked* back and screeched. The goblin dropped the baskets and took two steps to the side. He made four loud *clicks*, and then stood waiting.

Moss put down his basket, stepped closer to the goblin, and swung his cudgel, smashing it down on the horned helmet. The helmet, the goblin's head, and the cudgel all broke. Moss threw the broken cudgel to one side, bent down, and pulled out the goblin's sword and concealed it beneath his rags.

'Follow me,' said Moss, lifting his basket again.

'I think I must have called that goblin a rude name or something,' said Maddie. 'Wonder what I said.'

Roger just shook his head and followed Moss out of the passage and into the light.

The courtyard was busy with goblins scurrying about carrying bundles of weapons and shields, loading them on to handcarts. Sir Hugo was sitting on a huge throne perched on top of a narrow, circular balcony on one of the towers. He was howling orders through something fashioned like a loudhailer. There was a bowl resting on his knees and, between shouts, he was ladling spoonfuls from it into his mouth. The throne he was on was so tall that there was a little set of steps leading up to it.

'We're going to have to go underneath that balcony,' said Roger. 'He'll see us.'

Moss grunted. 'Keep your faces covered and follow my lead. I am a master of deception.'

Moss strode out across the courtyard, followed by Roger and Maddie; he was holding his basket as if it contained a great weight. He stopped suddenly, placed his basket on the ground, and began to examine the rags inside it.

'What are you doing?' hissed Roger, not quite believing what he was seeing. 'What are you looking for? What's wrong?'

'Nothing,' replied Moss, standing upright, and picking up his basket again. 'This is where my great acting skills are used. I am making myself as one with the enemy. I am looking to see if my clothing is clean enough to wear or if it requires further washing.'

'Don't,' said Roger, trying to keep calm. He wanted to run. 'Please don't. Please, hurry up, before they see who we are. Please!'

'Move,' hissed Maddie, her face buried under a pile of rags. 'Or I'm going to be sick right here. This stink is killing me. Talk about burnt toast. This is burnt sick!'

Moss, singing a washing shanty, walked over to the balcony where Sir Hugo was sitting. He passed underneath it and carried on to the drawbridge, sauntering past the guards. Roger and Maddie followed him with their heads bowed. The guards ignored them.

'We did it!' whispered Roger, as they stepped off the far end of the drawbridge. 'I can't believe—'

'*Leaving already!*' shouted a voice behind them.

Roger and Maddie turned.

Sir Hugo was standing on the balcony staring down at them. 'Thought it was you,' he shouted through his loudhailer. 'No one sings joyfully in this world. I banned it right after I banned laughing aloud in public places. *Guards!*'

Roger, Maddie and Moss started running as a horn sounded behind them.

CHAPTER
Twenty-one

'Oldest trick in the manuscript,' yelled Moss as he barrelled through three goblins standing in his way. 'You two should not have turned when he shouted.'

Roger thought of arguing back, but Sir Hugo's voice could be heard bellowing orders and horns were blowing.

As they ran, Roger and Maddie tore off their rags and threw them away. A few startled goblins scampered out of the road as Moss, waving sword and axe, charged past them.

Roger saw that the spider stable was just ahead. 'Make for the furthest wagon,' he shouted.

Moss was first to arrive. The wagon was being loaded with bundles of spears by several pale-skinned goblins, watched by a horned goblin leaning on a huge double-headed axe. As the horned goblin turned to see what the commotion was, Moss ran him through with his sword, and grabbed the axe before it hit the sand. The pale goblins scattered, squealing in terror.

'Get on,' shouted Moss, 'while I delay the pursuit.' He turned and swung the huge axe at the second wagon in the line, cutting through the supports for the runners. The wagon toppled onto its side.

Moss whooped. 'This is a fine weapon. I'll wreak havoc with this.' He jumped onto the first wagon and swung the axe round his head. 'I name this *Goblaxe*!'

Roger heaved himself onboard, then turned to help Maddie. As he pulled her up he couldn't help thinking that, as scary as Moss looked, standing there bellowing and waving his new axe, he wasn't nearly as fearsome as he had been with his beard and moustache.

'Drive the wagon, Roger,' said Moss. He shoved the huge axe into the sheath on his back and began undoing one of the bundles of spears.

Roger hurried forward and grabbed the reins. He stood holding them for a moment. 'Ready!' he yelled, and pulled. Nothing happened. He pulled harder. Still nothing. 'Umm . . . Go? Mush? Giddy-up?' he tried.

'Hurry up, boy!' bellowed Moss, throwing spears at any goblin daring to show its face. 'They will be upon us sooner than you could blow a fluffkin from a dandelion.'

Roger pulled again, then leaned over and looked down beneath the wagon. He could see movement as the spider's legs rippled in the sand. 'It's there,' he said, 'but it's not moving for me, Moss.'

'Shout *giddy-up* again!' yelled Maddie, standing in the middle of the wagon. 'But hurry up, they're coming!'

'Out of my way,' said Moss. He grabbed the reins and pushed Roger to one side. He leaned over the front of the wagon and jabbed a spear, several times, into the sand.

There was a terrible high-pitched squealing sound and the spider burst out of the sand and started running. There was a gooey white substance oozing from its body where the spear had struck it.

The wagon shot forward. Moss toppled backwards, dropping the reins and sending Roger and Maddie flying. All three of them rolled to the back, where they lay, clinging on for dear life, as the wagon sped off at break-neck speed.

'*Whajadothafor?*' screamed Roger, as they careered wildly, swinging from side to side, bundles of spears bouncing out of the wagon.

'*Fastgettaway!*' Moss ducked as spears flew over his head and scattered on the sand.

'*Stopit!*' screeched Maddie, just managing to hold on as she bounced up and down in the wagon. Moss grabbed her by the arm to steady her.

The wagon thundered on, juddering dangerously, its

speed increasing as it swerved off the track onto the open sand. There was hardly any dust this time; they were travelling too fast. Stones and rocks rattled against the wagon as it bounced along. Roger's body was rising off the wagon with each bump and the strain on his arms was tremendous; he wasn't sure he could hang on much longer.

The giant spider raced on, getting faster.

'Loo-look!' yelled Roger. 'We-we're-ba-back-where-we-came-in.' They were heading towards fields of bamboo and gnarled tulips. Just beyond the fields lay the goblin village.

They ploughed into the bamboo canes, ripping them apart – there was a brief pause – then they hit the gnarled tulips, tearing through them. The undamaged flowers on either side of the careering wagon started shooting water bubbles into the air.

'We must depart from this wagon with some haste.' Moss tried to nod at something at the front. They were heading directly at the goblins' stone houses.

Moss released his grip on the side of the wagon and wrapped both arms round Maddie. The wagon swung hard left. Moss and Maddie were flung out as it swung back again. They hung in the air for a second, and then disappeared from sight.

Roger could see goblins running out of the way as the

spider raced between the first houses. He closed his eyes and let go. There was a jolt, then a sensation of floating, followed by crunching thump as he hit soft sand.

He opened his eyes and raised his head. Directly in front of him the wagon piled into a goblin house. The impact smashed the wagon, and pieces of bamboo splintered off as it toppled onto its side and came to a shuddering stop. The giant spider, screeching loudly, disappeared into the desert with the broken reins trailing behind it.

'Hurry!' roared Moss. 'They're approaching.'

Roger looked down at himself. He was half buried in soft sand with only his legs sticking out.

'Quickly, Roger,' yelled Maddie, dropping down beside him and scooping out sand with her hands. 'They're coming.'

With Maddie's help, Roger pulled himself out and stood trying to brush himself down.

'What are you doing, you poop-noddy?' Moss's voice boomed. 'This is no time to see if your breeches are clean.'

Roger turned round. Moss was standing looking at him; the axe was now resting on his shoulder.

'Oh . . . just . . . go and boil your . . . pop-nodding-lip-clapping-snotter-clouting . . . whatever! I'm coming!' Roger stuck out his tongue and blew a loud raspberry.

'He has become addlepated,' said Moss. 'He is gibbering and making weird noises.'

'You OK?' said Maddie, looking anxiously at Roger. 'You hit the ground hard.'

'Yeah, thanks,' said Roger, and he grinned. 'Just a touch turn-giddy.'

'Ah,' said Moss. 'I was thinking that same thought. Now move.'

A very large dust cloud was approaching.

Roger started running. It was difficult to move in the blazing suns; the intense heat seemed to drain the strength from his legs, he had to force himself forward.

'When we reach the . . . beast,' puffed Moss, as they toiled up the slope from the village, 'I'll engage it in combat . . . while you two enter the portal.'

Roger, too exhausted and hot to reply, just nodded.

Maddie slowed down, and pointed. 'What's . . . what's it doing?'

'Watching . . . us.' Roger could see that the crocodile-beast was lying on the ground directly in front of the twinkling portal.

Moss lifted the axe from his shoulder. 'Be ready to go round when the battle commences. And be quick in your movements.'

They crept closer to the crocodile-beast. It slowly

stood up, stretching its four great legs on both sides of its body.

'Look at it,' breathed Maddie. 'It's just watching us.'

'When I am within its range, it will pounce.' Moss pawed the ground. 'Be alert.'

Roger and Maddie spread out on each side of the crocodile-beast.

'What are you going to do, Moss?' asked Roger. 'You won't defeat that! It's gigantic! It'll eat you!'

'Fear naught,' said Moss, walking forward, 'I have the measure of this tiddling.'

'Moss, stop,' shouted Maddie.

'Six more strides, Mad-one,' said Moss, counting. 'One, two . . .'

On the sixth step forward Moss stopped. With its mouth wide open, the great beast came thundering down the slope.

Moss stood calmly, holding Goblaxe in both hands.

Roger could barely watch.

There was a loud *clunk*, immediately followed by a terrible squealing and rattling.

The crocodile-beast was being yanked back by the chain around its neck. It crashed upside-down on its back and lay gasping with its claws waving in the air.

Moss walked forward, swung his axe, and buried it

deep in the creature's throat. There was a gurgling noise, then silence.

Roger cautiously approached Moss and the dead beast. 'How did you know where to . . .?'

'To stop,' finished Maddie. 'How did you know you were safe?'

'I have told you this already,' said Moss, sounding irritated as he wiped the blade of the axe in the sand. 'Do you not hear when I speak? I had its *measure* – the measurement of its maximum running distance. You can see by the marks on the ground the distance it can reach.'

'But . . .' began Roger, 'you might have got it wrong.'

'Or it might have broken the chain,' said Maddie.

Moss shrugged. 'Did not happen.' He pointed down the slope with his axe. 'Now you must go. The goblins are nearly upon us. I will fight them with Goblaxe and give you time to destroy the dodecahedron.'

'Don't be silly,' said Roger. 'Come with us, there's no need to stay behind, we can all go through together.'

'I have told you,' snapped Moss. 'I cannot return like this.' He pointed at his face. 'Go, now, before it is too late, they are nearly upon us.'

'But there is no need—' Roger stopped as Maddie gripped his arm and squeezed it hard.

'No,' said Maddie, giving Roger a wink. 'Moss is quite right. No one should see him like this.' She gave a shudder. 'Ugh! I mean look at him. He's ugly! Far better that he dies fighting than be seen without his beard. That would be crazy!'

'You see,' said Moss, 'Mad-one understands. Now go.'

'OK, goodbye, Moss.' Maddie pulled Roger up to the portal. She gave him a very obvious wink. 'Say cheerio to Moss, Roger. You'll never see him again.'

'Ehm . . . goodbye, Moss,' said Roger, confused.

'We're off then,' said Maddie, standing directly in front of the portal. 'Bye, Moss, hope you—' Maddie gasped. 'Oh, no! Will you look at that, Roger? The portal is broken. We won't get home. Oh, *boo-hoo, boo-hoo . . .*'

'Broken!' Moss pushed them aside. 'Where . . . how can it be broken?'

'There,' said Maddie, pointing vaguely, 'down at the bottom, there.'

Moss bent over and squinted at the lower end of the portal. 'I cannot—'

'*Now!*' yelled Maddie.

Roger and Maddie ran at the dwarf – and shoved him head-first through the portal.

'Male dwarves, eh, what are they like?' Maddie took Roger's hand. 'Ready?'

'Yes,' said Roger. He smiled. 'Let's go home.'

They ran at the portal, jumped through and landed on . . .

CHAPTER
Twenty-two

. . . grass.

Roger looked at the beautiful, green grass. It was wet, trampled on, and quite muddy – but it was beautiful. It was daylight and there was a wind blowing; a lovely cold wind. The flag on the golf course beyond the stream was flapping in the breeze. He looked up at the sky. Clouds!

Someone was shouting. Roger quickly let go of Maddie's hand as Lady Goodroom crashed into them and swept them off the ground.

'Oh, oh, oh!' Lady Goodroom hugged them tighter. 'Oh my dears, my dears, I've been so worried about you. William was just going in to find you, when the Captain popped out – then you! Oh, I'm so pleased you're all right. You should never have gone off by yourselves. I'd never have let you if I hadn't been under that mind-spell. Thank goodness William brought me out of it. *Ooh,* I can't tell you how happy I am to have you back again.'

'You're squashing me,' gasped Maddie.

Lady Goodroom dropped Roger and Maddie, and stepped back to look at them. 'Well I never!' She put her hands on her hips and stared at them. 'You're absolutely filthy! And you smell awful. What a state you're in! How on earth did you get like that? Pen, Pen! Come and see this. I'll need to hose them down with a pressure washer to get that dirt off. And your Halloween costume's ruined, Roger.'

Lord Goodroom and Wullie were standing arguing with Moss, who was shaking Goblaxe at them.

'Good morning!' shouted Wullie. 'Nice tae have you back. We're just trying tae talk some sense into the wee fella here. He wants tae go back in there just because he's had a shave.'

'I did not have a shave,' bellowed Moss, walking over to Lady Goodroom. 'Who, in their own brain, would wish to look like *this*?' He fluttered his fingers around his face. 'My appearance is hideous to behold.'

'Ach, I wouldn't go that far, son,' said Wullie. 'I mean, you were never any great shakes. In fact, truth be told, you were a right ug—'

'*Stop!*' Roger shouted as loudly as he could.

Everyone stopped talking and looked at Roger.

'Right, thank you,' said Roger. He pointed at the shimmering portal. 'Redcap is dead, but goblins are going

178

to come through there any second now. We've got to stop them!'

'It's all taken care of, Roger,' said Wullie, walking over to Roger. 'Have a look at this.' He led Roger to the side of the portal on the rock-face. There were boxes of fireworks piled against the stone, below the dodecahedron keyhole, and several rockets and more fireworks were tightly packed into the keyhole. 'There you are, all ready to go. And I put down a fuse-wire just before you arrived.'

'Will fireworks be enough to blow up the rock and the doh-doh-thing?' asked Roger.

'Aha,' said Wullie, tapping his nose. 'There's also a wee secret ingredient in there.'

'It's behind the fireworks that Pen bought,' said Lady Goodroom. 'High explosive.' She lowered her voice. 'William's friend supplied it, and Pen collected it. The fireworks are just a cover. It's Bonfire Night in a few days. What's more, Queen Gwri is trying to send us some help. But the dwarf army is in Greenland dealing with some troublesome polar dragons who have been drinking the volcanic lava again. And apparently dwarf wizards need time to make the magic to transport large numbers of troops.'

Moss nodded. 'I have the understanding of that. Did my Queen contact you by vole?'

'No, by phone,' said Lady Goodroom. 'We've started using mobiles now, can't always get a signal, but when we can it's much quicker.'

'So you see,' said Lord Goodroom. 'There's nothing to worry about, old chap, it's all taken care of. Just light the fuse and retire to a safe distance. *Bang!* No more dodecahedron key, no more portal. And help is on its way.'

'We were just waiting for you to come out,' said Lady Goodroom. 'As I say, William was just about to go in with a rope round his waist, when out you all popped.' She grabbed hold of Maddie and hugged her again. 'I really don't know how you got so dirty, you must have been rolling in something.'

'Was there a time difference where you were?' asked Lord Goodroom. 'Different worlds may not operate on the same time scale. If you know anything about—'

'I'm sorry for interrupting!' Roger spoke sharply again. 'But can we talk about this later? We should blow it up, *now*. You really, really don't want to see what's coming through there. Please, can we blow it up?'

'You are quite right, Roger,' said Lord Goodroom. 'Listen to me prattling on as if we've got all day. Let's get it done, and then we can all get home for a nice cup of tea.' He looked around at everyone. 'Who is going to do the honours then?'

'I am,' said Wullie, stepping smartly forward. 'I've been trained for this. You lot get way, way back.' He pointed down to the stream. 'Cross over there and get onto the golf course; that should be far enough, you should be safe over there.'

'I will light the fuse,' said Moss. 'You go to the safe distance, Wullie.'

'No,' said Maddie. 'Don't let him do it. He'll blow himself up.'

'Oh, please,' said Roger. 'Let's just do it. *I'll do it!*'

'I'm doing it!' snapped Wullie. 'And that's final. My explosives. Mine!' He held out his hand to Lord Goodroom. 'Lighter, please, your Lordmanship.'

'Ehm, I don't have a lighter, old bean. Don't smoke.'

'Matches?'

Lord Goodroom shook his head.

Wullie looked at Lady Goodroom.

Lady Goodroom shook her head.

'Ah,' said Wullie, and he turned to Moss. 'You smoke a pipe, Mossyman; I know you do. Give us your matches, please.'

Moss shook his head, 'I have no combustion material in my possession. I use a baccy-pipe only during times of relaxation.'

Wullie looked back at Lord Goodroom. 'When you

bought all these fireworks . . . are you sure you didn't, by chance, buy a wee box of matches – to light them?'

'Didn't occur to me, old chap,' said Lord Goodroom. 'Never crossed my mind.'

'Oh, boy.' Roger looked down at the ground and muttered to himself.

'Look,' said Maddie, 'over there.' She pointed at three sturdy lady golfers, with trolleys, who had just appeared on the golf course on the far side of the stream. They were walking down a hill. 'One of them might have matches or a lighter. We could ask them?'

'Good,' said Lady Goodroom. 'Let's go and ask them, then.'

Roger stood quite still as the others followed Lady Goodroom who was marching smartly down the hill.

'Come on, Rog,' shouted Maddie. 'Keep up. You might miss some fun.'

Roger sighed deeply and began walking.

'I say, excuse me ladies,' shouted Lady Goodroom, reaching the edge of the stream across from the golf course. 'I wonder if you could help us, please?'

The three golfers looked over. 'We are in the middle of a competition here, you know,' shouted back the smallest of the three ladies.

'So sorry,' said Lady Goodroom. 'It's just that I need

to ask you something. It's important. Won't keep you but a moment.'

The small lady spoke to her companions. They nodded their heads, and all three left their trolleys and walked down to the stream.

'Now,' said the small lady, looking suspiciously at the gathering on the other side, 'what's this all about? And just so you are aware, I'm the Lady Captain, Ms Katie Kettlewell, and you're interrupting a very important competition.'

'We're first out,' said another of the ladies, pointing her thumb over her shoulder. 'But there'll be more coming over that hill very soon, I can assure you.'

The third lady golfer just glared at them through thick spectacles.

'I'm most dreadfully sorry for interrupting your competition,' said Lady Goodroom. 'I'm Lady Gwendolena Goodroom, and that's Lord Goodroom, my husband.' She waved her hand vaguely. 'The others are . . . well . . . my ward and her friends. So what I wanted to ask you was—'

'*Lady* Goodroom?' said Ms Kettlewell, and she smiled.

'Yes,' said Lady Goodroom. 'Now, do you—?'

'And *Lord* Goodroom?'

'Yes,' said Lady Goodroom.

183

'Hello, girls,' shouted Lord Goodroom, giving a cheery wave. 'Nice day for it!'

The lady golfers smiled. The one with the thick glasses gave a slight curtsey.

'How can we help you, *Lady* Goodroom?' said Ms Kettlewell.

'Do you have a light?'

'A what?' Ms Kettlewell frowned. 'What sort of light?'

'Just a light, you know, a lighter or a match. Are any of you smokers?'

'I used to smoke,' said the lady with the thick glasses.

'You stopped years ago, Agnes,' said Ms Kettlewell. 'Why do you want a light? Is it for a nasty, dirty cigarette?' She narrowed her eyes.

'Oh, no,' said Lady Goodroom. 'It's for . . .' She looked back up the hill. 'It's for . . . fireworks. Yes, that's what it's for, we've got a whole lot of fireworks to set off, and we've forgotten to bring matches. Have you got any?'

'It's broad daylight,' said Ms Kettlewell, waving a hand at the sky.

'We like to be prepared, test a few, make sure they're working properly.'

'Bonfire Night is not for another five days.'

'Ehm, we're going away on a trip then, so we're having ours a bit . . . early.'

Ms Kettlewell whispered furiously to her two companions, and then turned back. 'Have you escaped from somewhere?'

Moss stepped out from behind Wullie and Lord Goodroom. 'Hear me you ong-tongued wallydraggles,' he shouted. 'Do you have *any* means of combustion in your strange-looking muckenders – or nay?'

The three golfers, mouths hanging wide open, just shook their heads.

'Then return to your game of swinging sticks at the ground and speaking of absurdities.'

The golfers just stood staring, speechless with shock.

'What now, then?' asked Maddie.

'I could go back to the village,' said Wullie. 'Wouldn't take too long to buy a lighter and come—' He stopped talking and looked at the three golfers. They were still standing in the same position with their mouths open. 'What's the matter with you lassies?' He laughed. 'The wee man is no that frightening looking. You should have seen him before he shaved his beard . . .'

The golfers began to tremble, their faces filled with fear and loathing.

'It's OK,' said Roger. 'We haven't escaped from anywhere. It's all right.'

Ms Kettlewell raised a shaking arm and pointed. 'No!' she shouted. 'Not here! Not on *our* course!'

Everyone turned round.

Horned goblins were pouring through the portal.

CHAPTER
Twenty-three

The goblins were wandering about looking at their surroundings: sniffing the air, touching the grass, gazing up at the sky. They all carried short swords and round shields, and were shivering quite violently as the cool summer wind blew over them.

'What *are* they?' Ms Kettlewell's voice was angry. 'What are they doing here?'

'Goblins,' said Lady Goodroom. 'They were here before, centuries ago.'

'Not that Yester Castle nonsense again, is it?' asked Ms Kettlewell.

'I'm afraid so,' said Lady Goodroom, looking a little surprised.

'So *what* are they?' asked Ms Kettlewell. 'Are they goblins or demons?'

'Oh, they're definitely goblins,' said Lady Goodroom. 'No question about it.'

'Well, at least you've cleared up *that* mystery.' Ms

Kettlewell sniffed loudly. 'I'm glad they're not demons, that would have been *really* awful.' She looked at her two companions. 'But it's still terrible, shocking – we just can't have goblins on the golf course, they'd ruin it! What'll we do, girls? If we stop now, the competition will be cancelled, and it's going to rain tomorrow so we—'

'*Who is that?*' yelled the golfer with the thick glasses.

A tall man had just stepped out of the portal. He was wearing a floppy hat with an extremely large feather in it, a gleaming silver breastplate over a loose black shirt, and shiny black trousers tucked into highly polished black boots.

'No idea,' said Lady Goodroom.

'That's Sir Hugo what's-his-name,' said Maddie. 'He's the one who cut off Moss's beard.'

'It can't be,' said Lady Goodroom. 'He died centuries ago.'

'And he's going to die in this century,' said Moss, hefting his axe and starting towards the goblins.

'Hang on a minute, son,' said Wullie, grabbing hold of Moss's shoulder. 'Don't go charging into that lot; there are hundreds of the wee devils, you wouldnae stand a chance.'

'Unhand me, Wullie,' snarled Moss.

'Think of the lassies,' said Wullie, taking his hand off Moss's shoulder. 'I'm no saying we won't fight them, but let's do it over there.' He pointed across the stream. 'Make them come tae us.'

'He's right, old chap,' said Lord Goodroom. 'We'd stand a better chance over there. You know, backs against the wall, that sort of stuff. And we would need weapons.'

'Very well,' said Moss, 'we make our last stand together on the other side.' He turned and walked down into the stream. 'Come, follow me.'

'I think that it's almost certain that we'll *all* be on the other side of something very shortly,' said Lord Goodroom, following Moss into the water.

'You there, *dwarf*!' shouted Sir Hugo, waving his sword. 'You cannot escape me. My army is on its way.'

Roger climbed up the embankment on the other side of the stream as Wullie and Lord Goodroom helped Lady Goodroom.

'My elite goblin bodyguard are here,' shouted Sir Hugo, 'dare you face them?'

'We stand here,' said Moss. He slammed the blade of the large axe into the ground.

'We have no weapons,' muttered Lady Goodroom, looking round about her. She turned to the three golfers. 'Can I borrow a seven iron?'

189

'Are you going to fight *that* lot?' Ms Kettlewell asked.

'Yes,' said Lady Goodroom. She nodded at one of the trolleys. 'All right if I help myself to a club?'

'But you can't fight these terrible creatures on your own!' There was a look of horror on Ms Kettlewell's face. 'You're only a handful – there's so many of them.'

'Needs must, I'm afraid,' said Lady Goodroom, smiling as pleasantly as she could. She nodded at the golf bag sitting on the trolley.

'Help yourself,' said Ms Kettlewell, turning to her friends. 'Well, you know what *we're* going to do, don't you?'

Ms Kettlewell's friends nodded vigorously.

'Come on girls,' said Ms Kettlewell, 'let's make a run for it!'

The three golfers began to run, very slowly, up the hill.

Lady Goodroom watched the golfers go, and then pulled a club out of the trolley and handed it to her husband. 'This will do you, dear.'

'Good show,' said Lord Goodroom, taking the club and swinging it a few times.

'I'll take a golf club,' said Maddie, pulling one out of the bag. 'You want one, Roger?'

'I suppose so,' said Roger, taking what Maddie handed to him. 'What's this?'

'It's a six iron,' said Maddie. 'I've got—'

'Look!' said Wullie, pointing at the portal. A goblin had just appeared and was looking around cautiously. The goblin ran to Sir Hugo, and began whispering in his ear. The goblin finished, and then ran back to the portal and jumped through.

'There we are, then,' shouted Sir Hugo, rubbing his hands together, 'all settled.' He smiled, pulled out his sword, and waved it at Roger and his friends. 'My advance column is arriving very soon, with the main army just behind. So here's what we are going to do; we are going to come over there and kill all of you. It'll get them ready, bit of practice, before the real slaughter begins.' He looked up at the sky and took a deep breath of air. 'It's so nice here. Much better than that burned-out crust I've been on for the past— Do you know, I can't remember how long I've been away?' He looked round. 'Where's my castle? It should be around here somewhere.'

'Stop cackling and face me nose-to-nose, you whiteliver,' bellowed Moss, shaking his axe.

Sir Hugo roared with laughter. 'With you, very soon.'

'On either side of me,' shouted Moss. 'Make ready for the onslaught!'

Sir Hugo started shouting orders. The entire goblin force lined up three-deep and stood to attention with their swords drawn and their shields to the front.

Sir Hugo waved his sword. 'Elite Goblin Guard – *advance!*'

The goblins began beating on their shields with their swords as they marched down the hill.

'Give me axe room.' Moss swung his huge axe from side to side. On his left stood Lord Goodroom and Wullie, and on his right side were Lady Goodroom, Maddie, and Roger.

Roger, gripping his golf club tightly, looked on in horror as the elite horned goblins neared the stream; the banging shields getting louder with every step they took.

'There's too many,' said Lady Goodroom, holding her club out in front of her. 'Roger and Maddie, when they cross the stream, you two run for it, get help.'

'No,' said Roger. 'I'll stay.'

'That's the stuff, Roger,' said Maddie, her face serious. 'We stick together no matter what. And I'm really sorry for teasing you – and calling you Rog.'

'That's OK—'

'*Not!*' said Maddie, and she chuckled. 'You're *so* easy.'

'Roger, Maddie, get out of here, at once!' said Lady Goodroom. 'Please!'

Roger looked at Maddie. She shook her head.

The shield beating stopped. The goblins had reached the stream. They were staring at it. Sir Hugo stepped out and raised his sword. 'Advance, goblins!'

The goblins were gibbering to each other, pointing their swords at the flowing water.

'Odd's bodkins!' screamed Sir Hugo, lowering his sword. 'It is just water. The stuff the flowers suck up. Look!' He walked forward, bent down and scooped some water in the palm of his hand and drank it. 'Mmmm, lovely cold water.'

Some of the goblins were shuffling backwards, breaking ranks. All of them were chattering excitedly.

'I know it's moving over the ground by itself,' yelled Sir Hugo, stamping his foot in frustration. 'That's what it does here you fools. It's not magic!' He looked down. 'Now look what's happened, my boots are covered in mud – ruined! I'd forgotten all about mud. Oh . . . it makes me so angry when the clothes I'm wearing get dirty. If it's not blood and guts then it's mud and dirt. And I haven't brought a washergoblin with me! *Oh!*' He raised his sword. 'Now, if you goblins don't get across there and start slaughtering . . . I'll . . . I'll do some *magic* on you!'

Some goblins took up their positions again, but most were still nervously shuffling about, staring at the stream.

Roger and his companions stood silently, watching.

Sir Hugo was about to call his orders again when a passenger plane heading to Edinburgh Airport appeared in the sky. His sword wavered in the air, and then he dropped his arm. 'What now?' he cried. 'What monstrosity is this? It is bigger than any bird I ever remember.'

The goblins were all staring excitedly at the plane as its wheels came down for landing. Some of them were clicking and a few were giving out little screeches.

'See its feet!' gasped Sir Hugo, as the plane passed directly overhead with its engines roaring. 'It must have a nest close to here; it is calling to its young. The worms it feeds upon must be enormous.'

Sir Hugo and the goblins stood watching as the plane disappeared behind some trees. He turned back and looked across the stream. 'And the eggs it lays must be bountiful indeed.' He paused, then raised his sword and pointed with it. 'And what sorcery is this?'

The gang turned to look. A small part of the hill behind them was shimmering. An elderly dwarf wizard walked out of the shimmer and looked around.

'It is the correct one this time,' shouted the dwarf wizard. 'Out you come.'

Nine heavily-armed dwarves marched smartly out of the hillside and stood glaring fiercely at the scene before them.

CHAPTER
Twenty-four

'So, you have summoned dwarf warriors,' shouted Sir Hugo. 'Are there more coming?'

'Scouting party,' bellowed Moss. He turned and winked at Lady Goodroom before continuing: 'The dwarf army is arriving just behind them!'

'You may be lying, dwarf,' bawled Sir Hugo. 'But in case this *is* the advance guard of the dwarf army and, with these fools unwilling to cross water without a bridge, we will withdraw and guard the portal until my vastly superior force arrives with the necessary equipment.'

He yelled orders. All the goblins snapped to attention, and then turned and marched back up to the portal, where they swung about and took up their three-line positions again.

The dwarf soldiers came trotting down the hill. There was a clinking noise as they ran.

'The Royal Guard,' said Moss. 'Queen Gwri has

sent my boonfellows to aid us. And Irongrip Knucklewood is at the front.'

'There's only nine of them,' said Roger. 'Will there be more coming?'

'Ten,' corrected Moss, 'I am their Captain. I lead them.' He dropped his voice. 'I have attempted a devious bluff. This is the entire Royal Guard. No more are coming.'

'But there's hundreds of them over there, Mossy boy,' said Wullie, pointing at the goblins across the water.

'You are correct, Wullie,' said Moss and chuckled. 'But now we can give a good account of ourselves. And dwarves always prefer to be impossibly outnumbered in battle.'

'Aye, right,' said Wullie. 'But there are so many . . .' He stopped as the nine dwarves reached them.

They were bristling with weapons: axes, daggers, swords, and each wore a metal helmet and had a shield strapped to his back. The dwarf wizard arrived, puffing behind them.

The lead dwarf stepped forward, banged his fist on his chest, and then stared in horror at Moss's face. He gulped hard before he spoke. 'We have been to three other golfing areas. The wizard had a difficult time with his projecting spell.' He leaned in and whispered hoarsely. 'Who did this terrible thing to you, Captain?'

Moss pointed at Sir Hugo, who was standing watching them. 'That human.'

The dwarves stared across the stream. Sir Hugo waved back. 'Is that all you've got coming?' he shouted. 'Not enough! My army will be here any moment now, with the means to cross the stream.'

'Tell me true, Irongrip,' said Moss. 'How is my appearance?'

'Hideous,' said Irongrip Knucklewood.

Moss nodded and looked down the line of dwarves. 'And what say you?'

'Fopdoodled.'

'Ugglied.'

'Gang-toothed.'

'Like a well used snotter-clout.'

'Um,' said Lady Goodroom. 'I don't like to interrupt this reunion, but we really do have to stop the goblin army – now!'

'Our army may not come soon,' said Irongrip, 'possibly several days away.'

'In a few days thousands of humans could be dead,' said Lady Goodroom. She looked at the dwarves who were standing watching and listening. 'Have any of you got a lighter or a match on you?'

'No one here carries the means of ignition with them,'

said Irongrip. 'I could, provided I have the correct stones and material, start a fire. Or any of us could turn stone to gold.'

'I'll bear that in mind,' said Lady Goodroom, frowning. 'But how do we get over there, *now*, to light the fuse, to set off the fireworks, to ignite the explosives? How do we get it lit without getting killed first?'

CHAPTER
Twenty-five

'I may have the solution,' said the elderly dwarf wizard, stepping forward.

'Speak then, High Wizard Turtledub,' said Moss.

'*Retired* High Wizard Turtledub,' said the elderly wizard, nodding his white beard. 'I have with me my greatfather's wand.' He pulled out a very ordinary-looking gnarled black stick and held it up. 'It is now but an ancient relic with almost no magic left in it. I keep it for sentimental reasons and it keeps my grand-dwarves amused.' He sighed, and seemed to drift into a happy memory, staring at the wand. 'But once all wizards used this. I think that they were better days, happier times. You knew where you were with a wand, none of this fiddling about with your finger-digit nonsense.'

'But what would you do with it?' asked Roger.

'Eh . . . what?' The High Wizard looked dazed for a second. 'Ah . . . well, human boy, I could set it to spark every few moments; there's enough of the old magic left in it to do that. *You* would just need to carry it with you, and touch it to the fuse to set off the display of pyrotechnics.'

'And I can get you there,' declared Moss. He looked at the nine dwarves, and pointed at Roger. 'This is the human known as the Destroyer, he is a warrior despite his puny appearance.'

'Aah,' said the dwarves, nodding.

'No, no, not me,' said Roger. 'I think he meant if *someone else* was over there at the rock-face. He didn't mean me. Not me! I don't want to go.'

Moss laughed. 'See, as I told you all before, he likes to make jocular remarks at moments of certain death.' He pointed at the goblins. 'Beyond them is where we must deliver the Destroyer.' He turned to Irongrip and the rest of the dwarves. 'Have you any thoughts on the best way to get there, in the quickest time? My choice would be, either a fist-crunch-leap, a covert-mouse, or a smell-the-smelly-pudding.'

Irongrip thought for a moment. 'A fist-crunch-leap,' he said. 'It has an immediate result against a shield-wall.'

'My thinking too,' said Moss, looking at the other dwarves. They all nodded.

'Good,' he went on, addressing Irongrip again. 'We are agreed on a fist-crunch-leap. Select your best leapers and I shall lead the fist-crunch. Leapers with battle-axes. Fist-crunchers with swords and shields. Make ready.'

'What's . . . what's happening?' asked Roger. There was a bewildered look on his face.

'We attack them,' said Moss, then he turned to the elderly wizard. 'Set your wand, retired High Wizard Turtledub, and give it to the boy, Roger.'

'We?' Roger looked at the dwarves getting ready. Some were stripping off weapons; others were bending at the knees and then jumping up in the air. 'You mean, you? *You're* going to attack all of them? The ten of you?'

'Of course,' said Moss. 'We attack them; all you are required to do is carry the wand and run with us. We'll deliver you to the fuse, and you blow the portal apart.'

'Is it safe for Roger?' Lady Goodroom was holding Maddie firmly by the shoulder.

'Of course not,' said Moss, who was being handed a battle-helmet by one of the dwarves. 'Extremely not safe.' He rammed the helmet onto his head. 'Could not be more dangerous. I cannot think of anything more dangerous at this present time. But there is nothing for *you* to worry about, Lady Goodroom, as you will remain here.'

'Do you want one of our battle-axes, Captain?' asked Irongrip.

'No,' replied Moss, sticking Goblaxe into the sheath

on his back. 'I now have a feeling for this mighty weapon. But I'll need a sword and a shield.'

'Can I go—?' Maddie looked up at her aunt and struggled against her grip.

'Absolutely not,' said Lady Goodroom, holding tighter. 'You'll be helping me with spells. And Roger shouldn't be going either.' She raised her voice. 'Can Roger not just follow on, after you've done your fist-crunching thing? Save him going now.'

'We may all be dead when we get there,' said Moss. 'And the Destroyer enjoys danger; he knows what he is doing. Besides, he is the only one who could keep up with the great speed of a dwarf battle charge. There is no time for any delay.'

'Are you sure you're up tae this, Mossy?' said Wullie. 'You've had an awfy rough time. Do you want me to step in for you? I know exactly where the fuse is.'

'Indeed no, Wullie,' said Moss. 'Your offer befits your bravery, but I am as fresh as a lamb at sparrow-fart time. And anyway, your leg-limbs would probably not stand the pace of the charge. Just give the boy and myself the exact location of the fuse.'

'See that wee tree, the single one, just behind the goblins on the right, there?' Wullie put his hand on Roger's shoulder and pointed.

'Yeah . . .' Roger could just see the top of the tree where Wullie was pointing.

'I see it, Wullie,' said Moss, nodding.

'It's just there,' said Wullie. 'That's where the fuse starts, you canny miss it.' He patted Roger's shoulder. 'Good luck son, you'll need it.'

'Tha . . . thanks,' said Roger.

Moss looked at Roger, and laughed. 'Did I not tell you that some day we might be lucky enough to fall in battle together as true warriors, brothers-in-arms?'

Roger found it difficult to speak. '*Mmm,*' was all he could manage.

'Well today could be that lucky day.'

'Gr-great,' said Roger, barely able to get the word out. Maddie was watching him. There was an anxious smile on her face.

'Positions!' roared Moss.

The dwarves moved into position. Three dwarves, holding swords and shields, stood shoulder-to-shoulder. Behind them, carrying battle-axes and spread out in a v-shape with three on either side, stood the other six.

Moss placed Roger behind the middle dwarf in the front row.

'Just run,' said Moss. 'I know you are a good runner.'

'I-I need the wand,' said Roger, glancing round

nervously. 'Unless it's not working, by any chance.' He could see Maddie and the others watching him; they all looked sad.

'Here,' said High Wizard Turtledub, handing Roger the wand. 'You just have to hold it. It's working.'

'OK. Thanks.' Roger took the wand and stared at it in trepidation.

There was a gentle *pffut* and a bright spark shot out, floated down to the grass and fizzled out.

'And, eh, human boy.' The elderly wizard poked Roger in the side. 'Return the wand to me when you are done, please. It is my most treasured possession.'

Roger nodded. The wand went *pffut*.

Moss marched round and stood directly in front of the middle dwarf in the front line.

'You fool!' yelled Sir Hugo, from across the stream. '*You're* actually attacking *me*?'

He shouted orders, and the goblins formed three tight columns. Each goblin stood with its shield overlapping the one next to him, and sword pointing forward.

Moss grunted. He raised his sword. '*CHARGE!*'

The dwarves charged.

Roger started a few steps behind the dwarves and had to run faster to catch up. He desperately tried to match the rhythmic *thump* as the dwarves' feet hit the ground at the same time. He had just managed to get the correct tempo going, when Moss shouted again.

'*Up-speed.*'

The dwarves began to run faster, feet pounding into the grass.

Roger could see the embankment and the stream ahead. The dwarves were breathing heavily; wisps of steam rose from their bodies.

'*All-speed!*' shouted Moss.

The running became even faster. Roger was flat out trying to keep up.

The dwarves swept down the embankment, splashed through the stream and up out the other side. Roger's feet were soaking, but he just felt great relief that he had made it so far without falling. In front of him he could see a solid wall of horned goblins crouching behind shields. They were all pointing their gleaming swords directly at him.

'*Leapers!*' snapped Moss.

The six dwarves on either side of Roger spread out and – one second they were there – the next, gone! Roger was vaguely aware of figures leaping in the air and dreadful swishing sounds followed by loud shrieks.

'*Fist-crunch!*' yelled Moss.

The four remaining dwarves raised their shields and ploughed straight into the shield-wall.

CHAPTER
Twenty-six

There was a *crunch*! The dwarves' charge slowed for a second, and then burst through the shield-wall. Goblins flew into the air. Roger tripped over a goblin lying on the grass. He stumbled forward, throwing out his hands to save himself. Something cracked as he hit the ground. A hand gripped his shoulder and he was pulled upright. He could see the dwarves moving about behind the goblin lines, swinging their swords and axes.

'Do not be resting!' roared Moss, swinging his fearsome axe and chopping through three goblins. 'To the tree and the fuse!'

'I wasn't—' Then Roger had a terrible realisation. The top half of the wand was gone. *It was broken!* He shook his hand. There was no spark from the tiny bit sticking out of his fist.

'To me!' bellowed Moss, taking out two more goblins with his backswing. 'Protect the Destroyer!'

Dwarves arrived, hacking their way through the

screeching goblins, and gathered round Roger in a protective circle.

'Onwards!' yelled Moss, leading the way again.

The dwarves pushed uphill until they reached the lone tree. Roger stuffed the broken wand inside the remains of his skeleton costume and looked for the fuse. The ground was a quagmire: chopped-up heather, grass and oozing mud where the goblins had been marching over it. There was no sign of the fuse.

'Have you found it?' bellowed Moss, as his axe sang through the air.

'No,' shouted Roger, ducking as bits of goblin flew over him, 'can't see it anywhere; must be trampled or pulled up. And I've broken the wand.'

'*You've done what?*'

'It broke when I fell – there's no more spark.'

'*Hunh!*' grunted Moss, slicing off a goblin's head. 'I would not like to be wearing your feet when the retired High Wizard finds out. It's been in his family for thousands of years.'

The circle of dwarves stopped moving forward. Above the screaming and clashing of steel, Sir Hugo's voice was bellowing orders.

The goblins stopped attacking and pulled back. The dwarves stood together, gasping for breath, looking at the goblins completely surrounding them. The ground was littered with the bodies of the slain; all the dwarves were bleeding from several wounds.

Sir Hugo stepped into the space between the dwarves and the goblins. 'So your army is *not* coming,' he said, grinning. 'This is all you have. How the mighty dwarves have fallen.'

'We have you beaten!' roared Moss. 'Do you surrender?' The other dwarves cheered.

'*I* do not surrender, you fool!' said Sir Hugo, walking slowly round the circle, looking carefully at each dwarf. '*I* am savouring the moment of your death. This is a moment of great joy for me.'

'I'll show you enjoyment!' said Moss, raising Goblaxe. 'Are you ready for a final victory charge, dwarves?'

'Aye, Captain!' roared nine voices.

'Then . . . *Kirkiema*—' Moss stopped as a tremendous screeching filled the air. Trumpets and horns blasted out in a fanfare of operatic music. Everyone turned to look for the source of the noise.

The crest of the hill behind them was filled with stout lady golfers. One of them raised a club in the air. A faint, '*Golf before goblins!*' could be heard, and then, '*Charge, girls!*'

Two grass-cutting machines and six golf buggies swept over the top of the hill. The operatic music was blaring out as they came on in a line together. Behind them the lady golfers ran. Some ran too fast and fell over themselves, and some stopped and sat down on the grass, but most made it to the bottom.

'What is that wonderful music?' Moss looked at Roger. 'It has a stirring quality.'

'Heard it before, but forget what it's called,' said Roger.

'Strong music,' said Moss. 'Has a goblin-slaughtering refrain to it.'

The music grew louder as the buggies and the grass-cutters approached the stream. The goblins were screeching and clicking excitedly.

'Shield-wall! Shield-wall!' Sir Hugo was running round, hitting out with the flat of his sword at the increasingly nervous goblins. He stuck his sword back in its scabbard, raised his hands in the air and shouted at the sky. Little flames ran round his fingertips.

Roger could see that Lord and Lady Goodroom, Maddie and Wullie had joined with the running golfers. The two grass-cutting machines, music blasting from speakers, had reached the stream, and were crossing without difficulty.

A bright ball of fire shot out of Sir Hugo's hands, flew through the air and hit one of the golf buggies on its roof. The burning buggy toppled into the stream, spilling its occupants into the water. A second, smaller fireball curved its way slowly towards another buggy. Just before it hit, the driver and passenger jumped to safety. The blazing buggy travelled on by itself and followed the first one crashing into the stream.

Sir Hugo waggled his hands again. A tiny fireball popped out this time, travelled a short distance, and then puffed out. Sir Hugo waved his hands for a few moments, gave up, and drew his sword. Suddenly his floppy hat with its feather flew off his head and soared into the sky.

Lady Goodroom and Maddie had stopped running and were standing with their hands raised. Even at that distance Roger could see that Maddie was laughing as she made the hat dive and then swoop in circles.

The other buggies, with shouted encouragement from the two wet golfers, crossed over the stream.

Most of the goblins were still in a loose shield-wall. But they were highly agitated, moving about nervously, jabbering and pointing at the advancing machines. A few goblins had thrown down their weapons and were creeping away with their hands over their big ears.

'Irongrip!' shouted Moss. 'Attack them from the flank. We'll go to the portal – see what we can do.'

Irongrip raised his axe in acknowledgement. The dwarves turned and ran back down towards the main goblin battle lines.

'Come,' said Moss, smiling at Roger. 'We go together, again!' He raised his axe and swung it at a goblin. *'Death or glory! Goblaxe brings death to goblins!'*

'Mmmmm,' mumbled Roger, ducking, as the top half of the goblin flew past him with a bemused look on its face.

Moss fought his way towards the portal as Roger, dodging round slaughtered goblins, followed.

CHAPTER
Twenty-seven

Roger and Moss reached the portal. They stopped, turned, and looked back down the hill.

The lady golfers had reached the ranks of horned goblins and were attacking. The two grass-cutters were ploughing into the three lines, scattering huge numbers and leaving wide gaps in the shield-wall. The four surviving golf buggies had stopped, and bright red fire extinguishers were being unloaded from them. As Roger watched, the lady golfers advanced. White foam from the fire extinguishers exploded over the goblins. The ladies swung their golf clubs viciously, battering down on goblin shields and helmets. As their golf clubs broke, the ladies picked up fallen weapons and continued the fight. Roger could see Wullie and Lord Goodroom standing in the thick of the fighting, swinging axe and sword at the goblin front line. Lady Goodroom and Maddie were at the back with the elderly dwarf wizard. All three were waving their hands and casting spells. A goblin suddenly shot up in the air, flew up the slope and crashed just in front of Roger and Moss. Maddie waved cheerfully at Roger.

Roger waved back.

Two more goblins flew out of the melee, both of them turning somersaults high in the sky before plummeting back to earth. Maddie waved again. Roger couldn't hear what she was shouting at him, but he raised his right hand and waggled his thumb at her in acknowledgement.

'Look there,' said Moss, indicating with his axe.

Irongrip and the dwarves were charging into the goblins' right flank. The nine were moving as one, chopping through the goblin lines like a thresher through wheat at harvest time. At the same time goblins were spinning into the air and crashing to the ground as levitation spells hit them.

The shield-wall – what remained of it – collapsed. The goblins began running, scattering in all directions.

'Now would have been the time to ignite the dodecahedron, Roger,' said Moss, watching the fleeing goblins. 'Are you sure that the wand is not working?'

Roger pulled the broken wand out of his costume and handed it to Moss.

'Hold this,' said Moss, passing his battle-axe to Roger. 'Perhaps the wand still works.'

Roger could hardly hold the axe, his arms straining against the great weight.

Moss shook the bottom half of the wand several times. Nothing happened.

'You are correct, boy,' said Moss, passing it back to Roger, who tucked it inside his costume again. 'It is, without doubt, broken. Any magic it possessed is now dead. As *you* will be when the wizard Turtledub finds out. Now give me back Goblaxe.'

But before Roger could move, a horned goblin, holding a spear, stepped out of the portal and looked at him with a surprised expression on his face.

'*All hasten!*' shouted the goblin, just as Roger, with an angry burst of strength, swung Goblaxe and knocked it back through the portal.

'*Unnnnnnnnng!*' cried the goblin, as he vanished.

'Well done, Destroyer,' said Moss, chuckling. 'You are indeed much stronger than you look.' He pulled out his smaller axe and passed it to Roger. 'Give me Goblaxe, and I'll keep any more of them from appearing on this earth.'

Roger looked at the axe Moss had given him. 'I've got an idea,' he said. 'Something you did before, when we first discovered the portal. It's a long shot, but it might just work.'

'Then do it,' said Moss, hefting Goblaxe onto his shoulder and standing beside the portal.

Roger looked at the dodecahedron keyhole; there was no fuse wire coming out of it. The keyhole itself was still stuffed with fireworks, but some of the boxes round it had been knocked over and fireworks were lying scattered and trampled into the damp earth. He pulled the remaining boxes directly under the keyhole again, kneeled down, and began hitting at the rock-face with his axe. Again and again he struck. Even in daylight he could see sparks flying, but none seemed to be landing on the fireworks.

'It's not working,' shouted Roger. 'The wind is blowing the sparks away.'

'Then it was not much of an idea.' Moss grunted, and there was a *thwack* sound followed by a shriek of pain.

'*Aaaah!*' Roger cried out in frustration. 'I thought it might work.'

There was no reply from Moss, just the sound of his axe: *Thwack! Thwack! Thwack!*

Roger stopped hitting the rock and glanced over. A goblin's head came snarling through the portal. *Thwack!* The head disappeared.

'If only you hadn't broken the wand.' Moss sounded a little breathless as he wiped some gore from Goblaxe.

'I didn't mean to!' Roger shouted. 'It was an accident.' He leaned against the rock-face, panting.

'Do not stop!' bellowed Moss. 'A Destroyer does not give up.'

Thwack! Thwack! Thwack! Thwack!

'I'm not a blooming Destroyer!' screamed Roger. 'And I'm fed up of all this! Every time I see you, it's nothing but trouble, trouble, trouble. I was sitting quietly in school minding my own business when you turned up spouting your usual rubbish.'

'I do not spout rubbish—'

Thwack! Thwack! Thwack! Thwack! Thwack!

'Yes you do! Trouble and rubbish! That's what you are!'

'My conversation is renowned for its brilliance and wit!'

'What?' yelled Roger. 'I'll tell you what you're known for—'

'Excuse me,' said a voice. 'Don't like to interrupt, but would this help?'

Roger spun round. Ms Katie Kettlewell, the Lady Captain, was standing there holding out her hand.

'Sorry the reinforcements took so long,' said Ms Kettlewell. She had something in her hand and it rattled when she shook it. 'Had to gather the girls and the

217

equipment, took some time to get it all together. Here!'
She rattled it again. 'Matches. I remembered you asked
for a light.' She shook her hand again. 'Just as well, eh?'

'Oh! Thank you.' Roger took the matches and looked
at them.

'I drove one of the grass-cutters,' said Ms Kettlewell,
smiling. 'Always wanted to do that.' She glanced back
down the hill. 'That'll teach them, spoiling our competition.'
She nodded her head. 'Shouldn't you get on with . . .
you know . . .?'

There were several more *thwacking* sounds.

'Do it!' roared Moss.

'Oh, right,' said Roger, opening the matchbox and
pulling out a bundle of matches. He held them over a box
of fireworks and looked at Ms Kettlewell. 'There's no
fuse; I think it's been pulled out or trampled. I'm just
going to drop the matches into this box of fireworks. It
might blow up right away. Hope not, but we'll need to run
for it. Really fast!'

'No problem,' said Ms Kettlewell. 'I go to Mature
Movers twice a week, I'll probably leave you standing.'

'Do it!' roared Moss, keeping up his continuous
thwacking.

Roger struck the matches and threw them into the
box of fireworks. '*Run!*' he screamed.

218

There was a *fizzing* noise, as Roger and Ms Kettlewell ran from the portal, followed by a *whooofing* sound. A ball of coloured light shot into the air.

'Run, Moss!' screamed Roger, as a rocket shot past him.

Moss walloped two more goblins back through the portal, turned, and began running after the others.

They raced down the hill, passing terrified goblins; rockets and fireballs zoomed into the sky and exploded with ear-splitting *cracks*.

'*Run, run!*' screamed Roger, as he saw the lady golfers and the dwarves just ahead of him.

Everyone began running.

A rocket shot between Roger and Ms Kettlewell and hit one of the golf buggies, setting it on fire.

The dwarves and the golfers splashed through the stream, past the two broken buggies lying on their sides, up the embankment and continued until they reached the bottom of the opposite hill.

Roger and Ms Kettlewell arrived at the stream together. Roger stopped running and turned round. Ms Kettlewell kept on going. The rock-face was a mass of flames, but the loud bangs had stopped.

'Has it failed to work?' asked Moss, as he pulled up beside Roger.

'I don't know,' said Roger. 'But the flames are dying down.'

'Then I shall return,' said Moss. 'Find out what has gone wrong.'

'I wouldn't do that if I were you,' said Roger, putting his hand on Moss's arm. 'It could still go off.'

'Fiddle-sticks,' said Moss, shrugging off Roger's hand, and beginning to run back up the hill.

He was about halfway to the portal when the entire rock-face and the surrounding area seemed to bulge. And then, a split-second later, the world exploded.

CHAPTER
Twenty-eight

Roger didn't really hear the explosion – what he did hear sounded like a muffled *crump* – rather, he *felt* it. He was lifted off his feet and thrown backwards into the middle of the stream. He lay on his back looking up at the sky as chunks of earth and pieces of rock splattered and splashed around him. A stone hit him in the chest, and he yelped in pain. Icy water was running over him, and his clothes were soaked through.

Roger rolled over in the water and scrambled up the bank. He was having trouble with his hearing. He stuck a finger in each ear and waggled them about, but it was no use, he couldn't hear properly. Roger gave up on his ears and looked around. The rock-face was gone; there was just a hollowed-out, smoking hole in the ground, and there was no sign of the portal or any living goblins. He looked across to the side where the others had gathered. The blast had knocked all of them to the ground.

There was a movement to Roger's right; a small bush

waggled and Moss staggered out from behind it. He was still wearing his helmet, but it was very badly dented. Bits of smouldering rock clung to his body.

'Moss!' Roger shouted. But all he could hear was a small fuzzy voice inside his own head.

Moss didn't answer. He was slowly turning in circles; his eyes were unfocused and his arms were hanging limply by his sides. He was unarmed.

Roger shouted again, louder this time. 'Moss!'

The dwarf kept turning. He didn't look in Roger's direction.

'Over here, Moss,' yelled Roger loudly, although it still sounded like a little voice deep in his head.

Moss stopped, and then began taking small splayfooted steps toward the golf course.

'No, this way,' screamed Roger. But Moss continued in the same direction with his strange walk.

Roger folded his arms round his body and stood shivering in his wet clothes. The people on the far side were getting to their feet again. Moss had stopped in his tracks, and was standing gawping at the hole where the rock-face and the portal had been.

Roger felt sore all over and there was a buzzing noise in his head, like an angry insect. He put the palms of his hands over his ears and pressed the side of his head several times. It made no difference. He was trying mouth-yawn stretches when he saw the hunched-over figure of Sir Hugo, creeping along the stream bank towards Moss. Sir Hugo's breastplate was dented, his clothes were shredded and smouldering, and there were wisps of smoke rising from his hair.

Roger opened his mouth to shout a warning, and then stopped. *Moss wouldn't be able to hear him.* He started running.

Sir Hugo bent down and pulled a small dagger out of his boot. Now he was gaining on Moss.

Roger bounded forward and launched himself at Sir Hugo's back. He missed completely, crashing into Sir Hugo's legs, knocking him forward onto the grass. Moss turned round slowly. His eyeballs were wobbling in his head as he looked at the two figures on the ground.

Sir Hugo jumped up, screamed silently at Roger, and raised his dagger.

Roger, on his knees, could only look up as Sir Hugo loomed over him. Just then his hearing returned.

'. . . ruined my goblinskin trousers!' Sir Hugo was shouting. 'How dare you!' He swung his arm back to drive the dagger into Roger. 'I am an immortal god!'

There was a dull *thunk*. Sir Hugo stopped with his arm raised in midair and slowly looked down at his chest. The point of an enormous barbed spear was sticking out of his breastplate.

Roger turned to see Queen Gwri, standing some distance away, her outstretched arm and hand still in the throwing position. Behind her, pouring out of the hillside, were armed dwarves. Icicles were hanging from their helmets and beards, and there was snow on their shoulders. There were also scorch marks on some of their tunics and armour.

Sir Hugo roared, 'How dare you! Look at the mess it's made.' He took a step back, and swayed; there was a puzzled look on his face. 'But – this makes no sense. I *cannot* feel pain.' He sank to his knees. 'But I can feel this . . . this is really quite sore.' He toppled onto his side. '*Very, very sore* . . . It cannot be, I am *immorrrrrrtal*.'

Sir Hugo twitched once, and then lay still.

As Roger slowly and painfully got to his feet, Sir Hugo's body began to crumble to dust. And by the time Roger reached him all that remained, swirling in the wind, were a few grains of reddish-looking sand, the barbed spear, a little pile of smouldering clothes, and two very dirty boots.

Queen Gwri walked over to Roger, on her backward-facing feet, and helped him up. 'The dragon spear,' she said, lifting it to rest on her shoulder. 'It destroys most things, but requires great training for accuracy. My apologies for the lateness of our arrival, but the army was in Greenland.'

'That's . . . that's . . .' Roger didn't really know what to say.

'Is Redcap dead?' asked the Queen.

'Yes.' Roger nodded. 'Though Sir Hugo killed him.'

'But were you present at his death?'

'Yes,' said Roger, 'both of us, me and Maddie.'

Queen Gwri lowered her voice and glanced around. 'Who removed the Captain's beard?'

Roger pointed at the ground. 'Um, him, Sir Hugo did it.'

Queen Gwri frowned. 'Then the trundle-tail met his end too quickly.' She nodded her head. 'You fought well.'

'Oh,' said Roger, standing a little straighter. 'Thanks.' He pointed at Moss who was wandering about aimlessly, humming to himself. 'What about him?'

'He is just a touch turn-giddy,' said Queen Gwri. 'He gets hit on his head a lot, many times much worse than this. It is but the tap of a feather on an iron bucket.' She smiled. 'Now, see, your friends are approaching. Go to them. My dwarves will clean the area. All traces of what has happened will be taken away.'

Roger could see Maddie, Lord and Lady Goodroom, and Wullie crossing the stream with some of the lady golfers.

Queen Gwri went over to Moss. She looked back at Roger. 'Have you and your friends received your wedding invitations?'

Roger shook his head.

Queen Gwri sighed and pointed at Moss. 'One task! That's all he had to do! Still, I suppose he has been quite busy. The arrangements will be sent soon.' With that she took Moss by the hand and led him away.

'Well,' said Maddie, in a loud voice, as she approached Roger. 'This is certainly the best, most exciting, Halloween I've *ever* had. Did you see Aunty Gwen and me? We were levitating goblins like mad. Took out stacks of them!'

Roger suddenly felt weary. He tried to stifle a yawn as he thought about his family and how upset they would be if they could see him now. He really was missing them.

Lady Goodroom was talking earnestly with Ms Kettlewell. The Queen and High Wizard Turtledub were gently leading Moss up the hill towards the shimmering hillside, with the nine dwarves of the Royal Guard following.

Roger pressed his hand against the broken wand in

his skeleton costume and turned away. 'Not even a hand-clap from Moss this time,' he muttered.

Maddie took Roger's hand. 'I don't think he knows which way is up.' She shook his hand. 'There you are, a hand-clap from me.' She smiled. 'You know, Rog, you really are getting the hang of this. You saved the day, again. With my help, of course. A *lot* of my help.'

'Don't call me Rog,' said Roger, smiling back. 'I've told you that I don't like it. And it was Ms Kettlewell's matches that saved the day.'

'Right everyone, time to go,' said Lady Goodroom, bustling forward. She turned and waved at the lady golfers. 'Fine woman that Ms Kettlewell. *Ride of the Valkyries* was an inspired choice of music to play when they came charging over the hill.' She looked at her husband. 'Unfortunately, too many of them are injured now. They've had to suspend their competition. I'll invite them to play at your course when they're all feeling better. And we'll have them over to Auchterbolton Castle for tea and scones after.' She waved again. 'Byeee!' she shouted. 'They're very happy, the dwarves have given them enough gold to pay for all the damage, and a good bit more.'

'Jolly good,' said Lord Goodroom. He and Wullie were supporting one another as they limped along. 'We were thinking of nipping back to that pub Wullie was telling me about. What was it called, again?'

'The Greedy Goblin, your Premiership,' said Wullie. 'I hear they do smashing bar snacks, although a *real* greedy goblin bought all their crisps and nuts to take home with him.' He laughed at his own joke and smacked his lips. 'And I could murder a pint or two, so I could.'

'Me too,' said Lord Goodroom. 'All that goblin bashing gives one a marvellous thirst.'

'No!' said Lady Goodroom, ushering everybody to move. 'Roger and Maddie need hot baths and dry clothes. And we need to get out of here, now! Before the authorities arrive to see what that explosion was. There'll be plenty of time for pies and pints later. And *I'm* never setting foot in that pub again. Let's go.'

'We'll have a few later,' said Lord Goodroom, laughing at Wullie's downcast expression. 'But I think we'll try a bar not frequented by goblins, eh?'

'Oh,' said Roger, as they set off, 'Queen Gwri said that we are all invited to her wedding.'

'Oh, goody,' said Maddie, skipping on the grass. 'I *love* weddings, nearly as much as I love Halloween.'

CHAPTER
Twenty-nine

'Have you seen the menu?' hissed Roger, during one of the many lulls, sliding the scroll over to Maddie.

'I'm starving,' said Maddie, taking it.

'Might not be after you read it,' said Roger.

'Don't care,' said Maddie, putting it down again without looking at it. 'I'm so hungry I could eat a goblin.'

Roger put a hand over his mouth to stifle his laugh, and then looked round the Great Banqueting Hall. He couldn't get used to the sight. The enormous hall was packed with guests for the wedding of Queen Gwri and Captain Mossbelly MacFearsome.

It was now several weeks since the portal had been destroyed and Moss, fully recovered from his injuries, had been ordered by the Queen to attend his own wedding. Lord and Lady Goodroom, Maddie, Wullie, and Roger had received their formal invitations, in which they had been instructed to pack enough clothes to last them several days, and to leave their suitcases one midnight on the steps outside Auchterbolton Castle for collection by dwarf porters. The following day the gang had driven to the village of Drumnadrochit. They had parked their car and taken a taxi to Urquhart Castle, overlooking Loch Ness. At nightfall they had been collected by hooded dwarves and bundled into a small wagon pulled by an enormous Highland cow. After several uncomfortable and bumpy miles, they had been led down a winding underground passage until they reached a grand entrance hall lit with flaming torches. From there, they had been shown to comfortable rooms where their clothes, hanging in wardrobes or neatly folded in drawers, were waiting for them.

Now, they were seated round a table near the platform upon which the wedding was to be conducted. Roger gazed upwards trying to make out the ceiling. The occasional worm or spatter of dirt dropped onto the table, so he knew that somewhere high above him there must be earth. The walls of the hall were decorated with garlands of flowers and intertwined tree branches, and the tables packed into the hall were too numerous to count.

'What's this for?' Maddie asked, kicking at a large brass pot on the hard-packed earthen floor. 'They're everywhere, round all the tables.'

'Oh . . . nothing,' said Lady Goodroom. 'Don't you

worry about it. Aren't the flowers beautiful, such a lovely aroma?'

'Tell me.' Maddie leaned over the table and stared at her aunt.

'I don't know!' said Lady Goodroom, looking away.

'Aye, you do,' said Wullie, slurring a little. He looked at Maddie. 'They're spittoons, dear. Once they get their baccy-pipes going, they can have a jolly good spit in them.'

'*Yeeeuch!*' said Maddie. 'That's really gross. I'm not going to sit here watching millions of dwarves spitting into buckets.'

'They also use them for being sick into,' said Lord Goodroom, also slurring slightly, 'if they need them. That's why they are wide at the top.'

'This wedding has been going on for an awfy long time,' said Wullie. 'Hours an' hours, an' hours. I think my kneeses and leggies and toeses have all gone to sleep.'

Maddie started giggling.

'Stop it, Maddie,' said Roger, trying not to laugh. 'The dwarves are watching you.' And then he giggled.

'Yes, stop it,' whispered Lady Goodroom. 'This is a *wedding,* it's not meant to be funny, it's serious.'

Maddie laughed harder. She stuffed a handkerchief

into her mouth and bit down on it, shoulders heaving. Roger, watching her, began to lose control. He turned away and put both hands over his mouth.

Lady Goodroom leaned back in a casual manner, and spoke to the table behind her. 'Weddings have this effect on humans, you know.' She circled a hand in the air. 'We can get very . . . emotional.'

High Wizard Turtledub, sitting at the table, didn't reply. He was staring miserably at the wand he was holding. There was a new bit of wood sticky-taped to the original bottom half. The other dwarf wizards at the table nodded politely and raised their tankards.

'Think I'm going to wet myself,' mumbled Maddie. 'Can't take much more of this.'

'What's that net in front of the platform for?' asked Roger, dabbing at his eyes. He pointed at the large stage, with steps on both sides, where all of the entertainment had been taking place. There was a tightly stretched net, strung along in front of it, just above the floor.

Lady Goodroom sighed, and took a sip of her robberwits wine. 'Do you really want to know?'

'Eh, yes, please,' said Roger.

Lady Goodroom sighed again. 'It's to catch the dwarves. A lot of them can be . . . quite intoxicated by the

232

time the dancing starts. They fall off the stage, bounce on the net, roll off, and then climb back up the steps again – if they can.'

Maddie started giggling again, quickly followed by Roger, then Lord Goodroom and Wullie. Lady Goodroom hid her own face behind her large handbag.

There had been a lot going on during the past few hours since the gang had taken their seats: speeches by visiting dignitaries, and a highly controversial speech from High Judge Turbid Syllabub outlining the proposed changes to dwarf laws regarding the fate of the human race. As Roger knew, humanity faced total annihilation in just 137 years for its continued destruction of the planet. The new law resolved to open talks with humans in order to solve the problems before the humans' time was up. During the judge's speech three outbreaks of fighting had to be brought under control by Irongrip Knucklewood and the Royal Guard before the judge could continue.

Then the Queen had paid a very moving tribute to Bloodbone Knottenbelt, and the entire gathering had risen to their feet and drunk a toast to the fallen warrior.

After that the gang had sat, mesmerised, as Moss and Queen Gwri entertained the gathering with a selection of ancient love songs, followed by a fifteen-minute clog-dance routine. Roger had timed it on his watch.

233

And then they had all sat, wide-eyed, as first Moss gave Queen Gwri a piggyback across a narrow beam covering the entire length of the platform. Then they had swapped places, and Queen Gwri, to much applause and wild cheering, had carried Moss back in the other direction. Finally, holding hands and standing on one leg each, Queen Gwri and Moss had hopped together, for five minutes, as the audience clapped in time. But now, with the build-up to the wedding over, all that was left was the binding ceremony itself.

'They're coming back!' said Lady Goodroom, clapping her hands as trumpets sounded. 'The binding is about to begin, pay attention.' She looked at Wullie and Lord Goodroom who were whispering together and laughing. 'Both of you, get ready to stand up, and no more merry-go-down until after the binding. Pace yourselves; there's a long, long way to go.'

Queen Gwri and Moss walked back onto the platform, followed by High Judge Turbid Syllabub. The judge signalled for everyone in the hall to stand.

Roger could hear several crashes as some of the guests keeled over. Two tables away a dwarf fell face-down, and then slithered to the floor, spilling wine, beer and cutlery.

'Now you know why they don't have tablecloths,' said Maddie, as the Royal Guard rushed about picking up the fallen and hauling them out of the hall.

'Be quiet!' snapped Lady Goodroom. She glared back at Lord Goodroom and Wullie, who were both swaying about with silly grins on their faces.

Queen Gwri and Moss faced one another at the front of the stage. They were bareheaded and wearing only long white smocks; their feet and faces were bare too. By now, Moss had regrown a rather short grey beard. Dwarf wizards had been working on it every day with spells and special unguents.

'What a lovely couple,' said Lady Goodroom, dabbing her eyes.

'Moss looks better like that,' said Maddie. 'Quite distinguished-looking. He should keep it that way.'

'Oh, it won't be long until it grows back,' said Lady Goodroom. 'And certainly not the normal years and years, about six months they reckon. I heard it's driving Captain Moss crazy.'

High Judge Syllabub raised his hands in the air and looked at Moss. 'Can you, Mossbelly MacFearsome, Captain of the Royal Guard and Protector of the Queen, marry this dwarf, Gwri Golmardottir?'

235

Moss cleared his throat. 'I can.'

The High Judge turned to the audience. 'Can anyone speak a reason why he cannot wed this dwarf?'

'*Because he's only got a fluffy-wuffy beardy-weirdy,*' shouted a drunken voice.

There was some laughter and some angry mutterings.

'I'll crunch you later, Rawhead Barleybank,' shouted Moss, in a jocular way, but with a strong hint of menace.

High Judge Syllabub glared down from the platform for a moment before turning to Queen Gwri.

'Can you, Gwri Fieryhead Mudgutted Golmardottir, the First of the Kingdom of Dwarves and the Protector of other Realms and Territories, Defender of the Innerland and Interested Party to the Affairs of the Upperworld (lest they ruin it by their insane behaviour) . . .' The High Judge stopped. He took several gulps of air before continuing, 'marry this dwarf?'

'I can,' said Queen Gwri.

The High Judge turned. 'Can anyone speak a reason why she cannot wed this dwarf?'

There was silence.

Roger jumped slightly as a worm *plopped* into Wullie's tankard.

'Very well,' said High Judge Syllabub. He kneeled down and, using a ball of black twine, started binding the big toe on Queen Gwri's backward-facing right foot to the big toe on Moss's right foot. When he was done he trimmed the twine with a large pair of ceremonial scissors.

Lady Goodroom sniffed and dabbed her eyes with a handkerchief. 'Love this bit,' she said, 'so romantic.'

There was another loud crash from somewhere in the hall, followed by thumping sounds. The Royal Guard rushed over yet again.

The High Judge placed a red ribbon over Queen Gwri's mouth and tied it at the back of her neck, and then did the same to Moss. He stepped back, lifted his arms high in the air and stood in silent contemplation for a few moments.

'This is it!' said Lady Goodroom. 'When they remove the ribbons from each other's mouths, they are married – at last!'

'You cannot walk,' said High Judge Syllabub, in a loud singsong voice, 'and you cannot talk –' he paused – 'without each other.' He looked at Moss. 'Do you, Mossbelly MacFearsome, remove the ribbon from your chosen companion's mouth?'

'I do,' said Moss, in a muffled voice, and he gently pulled the ribbon from the Queen's mouth.

'Oh, I can't stand it, it's so beautiful!' gasped Lady Goodroom.

Wullie took a long swallow from his tankard; he chewed for a moment and gulped hard. Roger looked at Maddie, who gave the briefest of shrugs.

'And do you, Gwri Golmardottir, remove the ribbon from your chosen companion's mouth?'

'I do,' said Queen Gwri, and she raised her hand to take the ribbon from Moss's mouth.

At that very moment, there was yet more commotion in the Banqueting Hall; a door was slammed and the sound of running footsteps could be heard.

The Queen's hand was just at Moss's mouth when a dwarf in armour raced through the Banqueting Hall and bounded up the steps onto the stage.

'Your Majesty!' yelled the dwarf. 'Captain! The Great Hall of Dwarven Ancestry has been broken into. Two guards murdered! The Grimspell Scroll has been stolen!'

There was gasp of horror in the Great Banqueting Hall, followed by a shockwave of wailing.

Moss ripped the ribbon away from his face. 'What?' he roared. 'Who did this?'

'A human was seen, Captain,' said the dwarf. 'A human who has murdered and stolen.'

'Call out the—' Moss made to move away, just as Queen Gwri shrieked and fell over, pulling Moss down with her. They struggled about on the floor kicking at each other with their tied toes and tangled legs.

'Oh, no,' said Lady Goodroom, and she plumped down in her chair. 'You know what this means?'

'We're for it?' said Roger, looking at all the angry dwarf faces glaring at them. High Wizard Turtledub was shaking his broken wand at him.

'Probably,' said Lady Goodroom. 'But it's worse than that.'

'How come?' asked Maddie, her eyes fixed on the tussle on the floor of the platform.

'I don't think they completed the ceremony,' said Lady Goodroom. 'I think that Moss may have ruined it. I'm not sure if they are actually married!'

'You mean . . .' began Maddie, pointing a finger at the struggling figures. 'That he's not . . . and that she's . . . not?' She pointed at herself. 'Does that mean that we'll have to . . .?'

'Exactly!' said Lady Goodroom.

'Oh, badgers' bums,' said Roger. 'Not again!'

ROYAL WEDDING MENU

NIBBLY BITES

Crispy pig trotters

Doubtful mushrooms with finely grated locusts

Deep-fried squirrel tails with red-hot chilli dip

Petrified fluttermouses with carrot jam

Quail eggs in anchovy sauce

Turnip soup (*Vt*)

BELLY FILLERS

Roasted chicken stuffed with garlic maggots

Angry Atlantic oysters drizzled in elderflower syrup

Minced maggot pie with moon-embarrassed tomatoes

Mushworm pie with peppered rodent tails

Crunchy lobster and deathwatch beetle skewers

Slow-roasted Aberdeen pork belly*

A turnip (*Vt*)

(*all Belly Fillers are served with unripe green potatoes*)

NUFFROOMS

Goat moths in whipped cream

Mandrake root with magic moments**

A trencher of hard stinky cheese

Tipsycake smothered in a beetroot compote

Frogspawn and custard

A small turnip with boiled water sauce (*Vt*)

Robberwits wine: red or very red   Merry-go-down ale

(maximum 7 bottles per dwarf)   *(unlimited supply)*

(*Vt*) Very tasteless

* With a bucket of tooth-snapping crackling

** Allow 6–8 weeks to recover

NO SHARP WEAPONS ALLOWED –
CUDGELS MAY BE WORN

ACKNOWLEDGEMENTS

Chloe Sackur, Commissioning Editor, Andersen Press
For her wisdom and prudent guidance this exceptional human
deserves sincere gratitude and wholehearted acclaim.

James Lancett, Cover Artist
An artist with the power of a wizard – his replication of my
rugged countenance is depicted in a most realistic manner.

Kate Grove, Art Director, Andersen Press
To control an adventure of such greatness within the design
boundaries of this book is a magnificent achievement.

Eloise Wilson, Fiction Editor, Andersen Press
Her dominance over squiggly-bits is absolute – it is remarkable
to behold the results of her expertise on a writing page.

Signed today,

Mossbelly MacFearsome

MOSSBELLY
MACFEARSOME
AND THE DWARVES OF DOOM
ALEX GARDINER

Roger's life is ordinary, until a grumpy dwarf warrior,
Mossbelly MacFearsome, appears out of thin air and saves
him from the school bully. Moss decides that Roger must join
him on his daring quest to defeat his arch-enemy Leatherhead
Barnstorm. If Roger *doesn't* help Moss, the world as we know
it will be destroyed and humanity will be annihilated.

If he *does* help, he will be late for his
tea and his mum will be going mad
with worry. A Highland castle, a
trainee witch who can do karate, and
an ancient spell to be broken . . . just
what has Roger got himself into?

'A rollicking rambunctious
plot and realistic characters'
Irish Times

9781783447916